THE BLOOD JEWEL

Book I
of
The Shomara Diaries

C. M. HENDERSON

Copyright © 2014 by C. M. Henderson
Cover design and illustrations by Marco Rano

All rights reserved. This book, or parts thereof,
may not be reproduced in any form without permission.

ISBN 10: 1495935612
ISBN 13: 9781495935619

Printed in the United States of America

DEDICATION

Dedicated to my grandchildren, Caitlyn, Ashlyn, Melanie,
Alex, Mia, and Lexi, for whom I have written my stories,
and
to my daughters, April, Mariann, Renee,
and my husband, Larry, for their patience
and constant encouragement.

ACKNOWLEDGEMENTS

As this book goes to print, it is largely because
of the support
and encouragement of many friends.
To those who took the time to read this book,
my mother, Wadene Adams,
Barbara Sorenson, Carolyn Giger, Marlon Browne, and
Fred Malir,
my heartfelt thanks.
Your insights and feedback have been invaluable.

Table of Contents

Chapter 1: DOUBLE VISION 1

Chapter 2: SHOCK AND SHAKE 8

Chapter 3: THE SPHINX THAT SCREAMED 12

Chapter 4: BACKYARD BOMBSHELL 17

Chapter 5: GIANT! 24

Chapter 6: THE MISSION 27

Chapter 7: KEEPER 31

Chapter 8: SPIRIT SIGHT 36

Chapter 9: SKY WORLD DO'S AND DON'TS 41

Chapter 10: FAMILY AFFAIR 47

Chapter 11: THE SURPRISE GIFT 54

Chapter 12: AMELIA STARFIRE 58

Chapter 13: SKY BATTLE! 61

Chapter 14: QUIRKS AND QUIPS 66

Chapter 15: CONFERENCE IN THE CLOUDS 70

Chapter 16: SLUMBER PARTIES 73

Chapter 17: THE REUNION 78

CHAPTER 18: PAIN AND CONFUSION 84

CHAPTER 19: THE CONFESSION 89

CHAPTER 20: THE GATE.. 93

CHAPTER 21: THE NEST 99

CHAPTER 22: RELIEF FROM AN ODD CORNER 105

CHAPTER 23: ESCAPE PLANS 107

CHAPTER 24: THE BIRD 110

CHAPTER 25: SHOMARA 115

CHAPTER 26: THE BLOOD JEWEL 123

CHAPTER 27: MARTIN'S SURPRISE 129

CHAPTER 28: TRANSPORTATION HANGUPS 135

CHAPTER 29: CRACK-UP!.. 141

CHAPTER 30: THE HIDE-OUT 146

CHAPTER 31: OUT OF THE FRYING PAN 150

CHAPTER 32: DANGER IN DISGUISE 155

EPILOGUE 160

ABOUT THE AUTHOR: 162

Chapter 1: Double Vision

"Life's minor frustrations can blind us to major shifts arising in our situation."
~Martin Moonglow

    Oh hi. My name is Barrington Arthur Klutzenheimer, Barry for short. Yeah, I know. Any parents with the last name of Klutzenheimer (that's pronounced *kloo-szen-high-mer*) ought be very careful when naming their offspring. Near as I can figure, my folks were off in another galaxy when I came along. It didn't help that, by the time I got to sixth grade, my body started acting up. No duh. No sooner did my toe stumble over a *painted* line on the gym floor than I would find myself spread-eagled in front of nine dozen kids. And I can't count the face plants in the school hallway that sent my backpack, papers and pencils skittering across the tiles.

    But the clincher happened in the lunch room. I had turned my head to look at Lupita Sanchez—and slammed right into a pillar. Try living that one down. And yes, my name did evolve. I became—yeah, you guessed it—Barry Klutzy.

    The fact that I have red hair that looks like a crop of rusty wires growing out of my head didn't help either. I tried to get everybody to call me Rusty but it never took. I guess Rusty Klutzy was not nearly as much fun as Barry Klutzy.

    But the day I had my first total meltdown was when I started *seeing* stuff. I remember it was garbage pickup morning. Get this.

Before I could even get my eyeballs open, my mom hollered outside my bedroom door.

"Barry, get up! I need you to take out the trash." Sweet wake up call, right? But it was breakfast when she lobbed her real grenade.

I was guzzling my orange juice. "So, Barry dear . . . . what are you doing after school today?" she asked. I froze, my juice glass still in mid air.

Uh, oh.

Finally I said, "Uh, nothin' I guess."

Wait for it . . . .

"Good. I want you to clean out the garage when you get home."

My appetite disappeared like pepperoni pizza in a football locker room. I stood up and headed for the stairs. Mom's voice snagged me before I got two steps.

"Barry?"

"Yeah?"

"You did hear me, right?"

Lemme think. No? Duh-h.

"Yeah, I heard you."

"No excuses, today, Barry. Getting the car inside is already hard. Now, with winter coming on, ..."

"All right, *all right!* Just don't bug me about it anymore, 'kay!"

"Barrington Arthur! What about that respect thing we talked about last week?"

I stopped with my back to her and rolled my eyes. "Yes, Mom," I said in my best "respect" voice.

"That's better," she said, "And don't roll your eyes."

Dang! How does she do that? She's gotta have hidden cameras around here somewhere.

I thought of my sister, Jenny, and growled all the way up the stairs. "Mom never makes *her* do anything except empty the dishwasher. But me? She gives *me* all the heavy jobs around the whole house! Ever since Dad . . . ." My throat tightened.

Dad, I really miss you. Oh yeah. I haven't told you that part. My dad was killed when his car nose-dived into the river six months ago.

Up in my room, I slid on my backpack. Then, returning the stairway, I boot-stomped each stair all the way down and shouldered the front door, letting it slam behind me. Mom yelled about the trash again, but I didn't look back. I just hauled up my bike, knocked the kickstand to the side, and peeled rubber all the way to the street.

School didn't help my mood. My best friend, Chad Sorenson, was away on vacation in Hawaii. Life was dull without him. I yanked open my locker, grabbed my books, and rammed the locker door shut with my elbow. *You scuzzball, Chad. How could you take off to Hawaii for two whole weeks? Here I have to go to these mind-numbing classes while you're stretched out on some beach in Waikiki.*

Ever since he moved here three years ago, Chad and I have been best buds. Chad is the only one who can make me laugh. Take the day he bought a bag of Cheetos, put two in his nose, one in each ear, and let two more dangle from his upper lip while he ate his lunch. If Mrs. Gimbal hadn't come over and made him take them out, he'd still be wearing them.

But today there was nothing to laugh about. In fact, everything made me see red. I saw Dave Dimmerwitz and two of his hoods up to their old tricks. They were harassing some new kid with coke-bottle thick glasses and a brand new backpack. "The Dave" was playing his favorite gag. He'd buy a can of soda pop and shake it real hard. Then he would walk up to a newbie, hand him the coke, and "welcome" him to Fairmont Middle School. I felt so helpless when the boy smiled and opened the can, only to have it squirt all over his face and his shirt.

I know the feeling. Without Chad here, I always feel like a neon sign flashing "Nerd Alert! Nerd Alert!" When I walk past the eighth grade homeroom every day, there's always a mob of kids hanging around the hall doors chanting, "There goes Brainy Barry!"

I hate that razz. Today, I swung around and walked backward. "Wha-a-at!" I yelled. "So now it's a mortal sin to make A's?"

Yeah. Okay. So I pulled a 3.95 GPA last quarter. Big deal. If it weren't for Chad, I'd let my grades slide. But we've got this bet going, see? Whoever pulls the best GPA for a quarter gets to give the other a noogie. Chad, the rat, made a straight 4-pointer. My head still hurts. But, hey. He's missing two whole weeks of school.

he can't possibly make up his grades now. Revenge will be so sweet.

Just then, Dave Dimmerwitz rounded the corner in front of me. *Dang. This just ain't my day.* He yanked me off my feet and bashed me against the wall.

"Hel-lo-o, Barry *Klutzy*," Dave said with a snicker.

He shoved his face in close and I choked. *Ew-w! Honkin' case of dragon breath there, Davey.*

He shook me and said, "Got a message for you so listen up."

Uh, yeah. Like I have a choice.

I did manage to mutter, "Why don't you leave me alone, you punk."

Dave pretended he didn't hear me and went on. "Me and the gang have decided that you're not makin' anything more than a "C" on that science test today. Got it?"

I nodded. It was never a good idea to argue with The Dave.

That's when I saw . . . . I felt my jaw go slack. *What the . . . ? No! It can't be.* But there was no mistake. Out from behind Dave's teeth crawled a mass of . . . maggots.

Dave scowled at me, his mouth full of worms, and mumbled, "You don't look so good, Klutzy." Then he snorted—and a fat maggot flew out of his nose and landed on my chin!

I went ballistic. I wind-milled my arms and clawed at the wall behind me trying to pull away. Dave laughed and swung me around pinning me against the lockers.

"Whatsamatterwichoo?" he roared. "Scared?"

I felt the worm drop down inside my shirt and I screamed. "Ee-yew-w! It's crawling on me!" I scrambled backwards digging my heels into the locker door.

"I'm not crawling on you," Dimmerwitz smirked. "Not yet anyway. But hey! Where's your bodyguard? Ol' Chaddo gone AWOL, has he?" Then he yanked on my jacket real hard. "Listen, Barry Brainiac, if you make an 'A' on that science test today, the gang is gonna bend your fingers back so bad you won't be able to hold a pencil for a week. Got it? You make the rest of us look so dumb."

Then he let me go. My legs turned to Jello and I slumped to the floor. How I wanted to smash that sewer rat's face! But after seeing all those maggots, I wasn't about to touch him. Besides, at five foot nine inches and a mere one hundred fifteen pounds, I didn't stand a chance against a pigmy, let alone a brawny brute like Dimmerwitz.

Then I felt it. The maggot! It was still down my shirt. Shuddering, I watched The Dave swagger off. As soon as his back was turned, I shot to my feet. You'd have thought I was auditioning for "Dancing With the Stars" the way I twisted and gyrated and flapped my shirt up and down. Finally, the worm dropped to the floor—and I mashed it with my foot.

"Yech-ch!"

In a state of shock, I still managed to get to the science lab that afternoon for the test but I couldn't remember why. My brain was still reeling from my encounter with Dimmerwitz. I kept seeing little slimy things slithering across my paper. It didn't help that Dave and his bozos kept giving me the evil eye all through the period. What I scribbled on that test was anybody's guess. I just wanted to get out of there. The moment class was over, I tossed my paper onto the teacher's desk and made a beeline for my locker.

And that's when I saw him. A tall man wearing a long overcoat passed me in the main hall not twenty feet away. Something about him made me stop and swing around. *That walk. He leans one shoulder to the right just the way Dad did!* My heart wore cleats climbing into my throat.

"Dad!" I shouted, but the man continued to move away, even lengthening his stride as he made for a side door. I dived into the after-school crush, pushing, shoving, bobbing above the sea of heads to keep him in sight. But the hallway was packed. By the time I reached the door, he was gone. I dashed outside. A long line of school buses stretched the full length of the block. I looked both ways. I even jumped onto the buses and scanned every face. But the man had just evaporated.

The soles of my shoes felt like lead weights as I shuffled back to the school. I slumped down against a wall and dumped my head onto my arms. *Dad. I'm never going to see you again, am I?* My face was soon wet with tears and I pulled my hood up. I felt myself go cold, then hot, then cold again. Ever since the accident I have imagined seeing Dad umpteen times. It ripped my heart out every time. Now with this maggot stuff on top of it all, I felt like my life was circling the drain. Nothing made sense anymore.

Then I wiped my eyes and slammed my fist on the cement. "I am *not* cleaning your garage today, Mother *Dear!*" I growled. The last thing I needed was time in that garage. The place was full of memories. Dad and I had spent many a golden hour puttering in that garage. It had been our playground. Dad would always start out with, "Hey, Barry. Mom's been wanting a water fountain. I've got an idea how to construct one. Interested?"

I was always interested. It was so cool to hang out with my dad. He had a way of making me feel important. And tinkering with him at his tool bench always yielded some fascinating insight. He would even listen to my ideas. Now . . . .

I swept my hand across my face and jumped to my feet.

"I need a place to zone out. Maybe I'll hit the video arcade." I called my mom's cell phone and her voice mail took the call. "Hey, Mom, I'm going over to Chad's for a while. See you at dinner."

Now I was well aware that Mom didn't know Chad was in Hawaii. I'd forgotten to tell her. Okay, so I told a little white lie. Big deal. But my mom *does* know that Chad and I are competing for good grades. Mom will just think I'm over at Chad's studying. She didn't know that we usually played video games in his rec room instead.

The real truth was, I hoped my mother would forget about the garage. After Dad died, she had gone to work full time. Her new job stressed her out and I knew she'd been really absent-minded lately. *Right, Barry. Why do YOU forget the problems your mom has to face every day?* Who said that? Yeah, okay. I do forget.

Uh-uh. You did not forget.

With Chad gone, my only option was the video arcade.

That is not your only option.

Yeah, but I don't have a rippin' game room like Chad's.

You know your mom hates the video arcade.

Okay, I knew that, too. It wasn't like she hadn't told me a hundred times. I could say her speech by heart:

"Video arcades are so unhealthy, Barry," I mouthed in my best 'Mom' voice. "Kids that hang out there are not the kind of friends I want for you. It's just not safe."

Of course, I always had my pat answer. "I'm street smart, Mom. I can take care of myself."

With that, I shut all my inner voices down hard.

In no time, I was savoring the sights and sounds of the arcade. Like any hard core gamer, I loved the noise of the place. It made me feel alive. I took my time wandering back to my favorite game.

But wouldn't you know, who showed up out of nowhere but Calvin Lumpskin, one of Dave's goons. Right off the bat, the guy stepped in front of me. I moved to go around him but he deliberately blocked my way again.

"Hey, dog breath. Let me through!" I said, trying to sound macho.

"Tell me you got no more than a 'C' on that science test, today," Calvin demanded.

I flipped my hair back. "Hey, how should I know?" I said. "In case you haven't noticed, the teacher hasn't graded our papers yet. Now move it!"

Calvin just stood there, arms folded across his chest.

I raised my voice and shouted, "Did you hear me, mush brain! Get out of my way!"

Lumpskin wobbled his head from side to side. "Make me," he said.

Okay, that's when I lost it. I hauled back and socked the jerk right in the chest.

What happened next was something out of a nightmare. A thick, spiked tail shot *out* of Calvin's chest and grabbed my arm!

The sudden pain stunned me. But when the tail began twisting itself around my arm, I couldn't hold back my screams.

"Awch-h-ha!!" Long boney spears tore right through my jacket and into my flesh. My knees buckled and I began to black out. In the far recesses of my tortured mind, I wondered why not a single head in the entire establishment was even turned in my direction. Did nobody hear me? Did nobody see what was happening?

I tried to tear the spikes away with my other hand but the hideous tentacle gripped even tighter. Lights began flashing in front of my eyes and panic gripped my throat. I jerked my head up to shout at Lumpskin—and froze.

Calvin Lumpskin was not there. Instead, mere inches from my nose, a grisly beast stood drooling over me.

CHAPTER 2: SHOCK AND SHAKE

"Life sometimes takes a drastic change of direction. In these watershed moments, nothing is ever the same again."
~Martin Moonglow

Slivers of ice crackled through my veins and my breath came in short gulps. *Where's Lumpskin? How did this monster get here?* Parts of Calvin were still visible. His arms dangled uselessly like thick noodles and his legs looked like fat pegs glued to the floor. The only thing that moved was that wicked tail cranking its bony spines into my arm.

I stared up at the brute. Eyes full of hate glared down at me from under haystack eyebrows. Its head was an oversized blob, misshapen and lumpy with a pus-colored scalp that looked moist but scabby. Bits of frizzled hair dotted the crusty skull like sagebrush on the Mojave Desert. A scummy, orange tongue hung across jagged teeth. It's lips, dried and split were curled into a menacing sneer. Most disgusting of all was the smelly slime dripping onto my face.

Then high-pitched shrieks split the air. New heads, smaller versions of the large one, burst from the shoulders of the creature. The yowling skulls lunged forward on their skinny necks trying to get at me. Even worse, every mouth vomited maggots! They wriggled like live spaghetti. Gag! They smelled like a sewer. Then squirming worm clumps began dropping onto my chest. I screamed in horror, still trying to tear away the spiked tail.

All of a sudden the monster roared, "This brat's not one of ours! Look! He's so scared you'd think he could see us. We can really mess with this one." At first, my knees turned to water. Then something inside me exploded.

"Yee-AW!" I shouted—and jerked my trapped arm at the same time. Caught off guard, the creature let go. I was free!

Without a backward glance, I tore out of the arcade flinging maggots as I went. I dashed down the hall, rammed open the mall doors, and raced for my bike. Fumbling for the padlock, I tried to open it twice.

No-o-o! Not now, Barry! You can't forget the combination now . . . !

At last the lock yielded and I scrambled onto my bike. I slammed down on the pedals so hard that the wheels spit gravel for three feet.

"I'm a stark . . . raving . . . *schizo*!" I wheezed, plowing my bike ahead with frenzied concentration. My chest heaved and sweat poured into my eyes. Every few moments I glanced back. Was it following me? I shuddered. I could still feel grubs crawling all over my body. Powering at full throttle, I blew through red light after red light and zigzagged through the traffic. Angry drivers, forced to step on their brakes, shouted at me above screeching tires and honking horns. I didn't care. I had only one thought. *I gotta get away. I gotta get away from that. . . that . . . that THING!*

Up ahead I saw a park. Jumping the curb, I scrambled off my bike and let it clatter to the ground. I tried to walk but instead, I stumbled to the ground with a muffled cry.

There I lay for the longest time, wanting to scream, but too traumatized to make a sound. Over and over, the scene at the arcade played in my mind like a never-ending horror movie. *Am I trippin'? Why didn't anybody come to my rescue? Surely any clown with eyeballs should have seen what I saw.*

"This is like over-the-top whacko," I moaned. "Stuff like this doesn't happen in real life."

It couldn't be true, could it? Dad always said, "Remember, son, there is always a logical explanation for everything."

I groaned. It had to be a psycho-trip. But even Chad's scariest video game paled next to this. How could this happen? Maybe my apple juice at lunch was tainted. Maybe somebody slipped a mind bender into my chili. Maybe the strobe lights at the arcade weirded me out.

A new thought struck me.

Hey! Maybe I'm home in bed having a nightmare, and pretty soon I'll awake up.

I sat up with a jerk, damp leaves still clinging to my shirt.

A terrible pain shot up my arm.

"Oo-ooh! Awyeee!" I howled and fell back onto the grass, hysteria rising in my throat. I forced myself to look down at my arm.

"No! Impossible!"

The sleeve of my coat was ripped and hanging in shreds. Through the gashes I could see my arm, gouged and bleeding. Even worse were the worms crawled in and out of the lacerations. My stomach lurched. Cringing I tried to pick them off one by one and fling them into nearby bushes.

Then it hit me. "That devil attack, the spiked tail—they're real! I have the wounds to prove it. I'm not crazy . . . or am I?"

Then I knew I was going to hurl. I jumped to my feet and rushed behind a hedge, hit by violent heaves. When my coughing and sputtering let up, I tried to stand but dizziness knocked me to the ground.

Get a grip, Barry. Use your smarts. Yeah, duh. I feel about a smart as a hairball right now.

I didn't know what was real and what wasn't. The grass under me was real enough, still wet from a recent watering. I could smell the damp earth; I could run my fingers through the wet autumn leaves around me. A squirrel scampered across the lawn and up a tree, chattering at a blue jay hanging from a branch above it. A very real cold November wind seeped through my soggy pants and set me to shivering.

But the pain in my arm was real, too. How I wished I *was* having a nightmare. Then I could chalk this up to "dreams I never want to repeat"–emphasis on *NEVER*.

But somehow I knew that this was no nightmare. Why, I couldn't say. I just *knew* this was different. I knew this was real life in real time.

I need to talk to somebody—anybody.

"Darn you, Chaddo," I muttered. "Taking off to Hawaii just when I need you the most." But then I stopped and ran my good hand across my nose.

What's the use? Think Barry. The truth is, you can't talk to anybody. A monster with a spiny tush? Worms oozing out of its mouth? Like, duh-h-h. Who's gonna buy that fairytale? Even Chad would toss that back in my face. As for my arm, he'd just say I wiped out on my bike or something. He'd accuse me of trying to milk a little sympathy. He'd call me a wimp.

As for my family—I rolled my eyes. Can't talk to Mom. Mom would go manic if she thought I was anywhere near the video arcade. And Jenny? I felt my lip curl. Jenny was a died-in-the-wool informer. I wouldn't tell her I had a toothache.

Maybe I should talk to my pastor. Nope. Bad idea. Pastor Peters would call the cops. I dug my fists into my eyes. Ugh! That was the last thing I needed, a roomful of people asking questions.

I slammed my open palm onto the muddy grass. "No! No questions!" I shouted to an empty park. "Not until I can get some answers of my own."

Then I saw the sun setting behind the trees and scrambled to my feet.

"Mom! I'd better get home before she misses me."

CHAPTER 3: THE SPHINX THAT SCREAMED

In times of confusion, we latch onto habits to steer us, habits that have served us well in the past.
~Martin Moonglow

I tried to ride home with great care but my brain was so elsewhere. My bike kept finding potholes. One time I nearly did a looper right over the handle bars. I thought my teeth would fall out! But my poor arm took the brunt of it. The jolt had me in tears. Finally, I got home and hid my bike behind the house. I crept up the porch steps, inched open the back door, and listened. Silence.

I sniffed. *Hm-m. Smells like roast beef. Mom must be in the kitchen.* I took off my shoes and, easing the door shut behind me, I padded into the hallway. Then I peeked into the kitchen.

Woo-hoo. Mom's not here. Now I can zip up to my room before she knows I'm home.

Gym shoes in hand, I began tiptoeing up the stairs. Out of nowhere my mother's voice blasted my left ear.

"Barrington Arthur!"

My hair spiked all by itself. Dang! Where *was* she hiding? The broom closet?

"Just where have you been, young man?" my mother demanded. "Here dinner's almost ready, and you look like you just took a mud bath."

Very good, milady. Thou art most perceptive.

"Oh, uh . . . h-hi, Mom!" I stuttered. I stutter when I'm nervous. I shoved my injured arm behind my back.

"I see the garage is still a mess and . . . ." Mom paused. "Why are you carrying your shoes?"

"Oh, um . . . they were muddy," I said. "Didn't want to get the floor dirty,"

"Uh-huh," said my mother in her infamous I-don't-believe-a-word -you're-saying tone of voice. "Well we need to discuss why you went over to Chad's and didn't come home right after school," she said.

Uh-oh. Mom's lips are goin' tight. I'm in deep doo-doo. I stared at her, unable to say a thing.

"Well, just don't stand there. Get yourself cleaned up. Dinner will be on the table in ten minutes."

"Okay. Uh . . . er, it'll just take me a few minutes, Mom." I turned away and sprinted up the stairs before she could say anything more.

I was almost at the top when Jenny brushed past me. She stopped and turned around.

"Barry . . . ?"

I pulled up short and looked down at her. "Yeah?" I said.

Jenny sniffed and squinted her eyes. "You . . . ." Then she frowned and said, "Oh nothing," and continued down the stairs.

I ducked into the bathroom next to my room.

"Aw-wch! My arm is killing me."

I stripped my torn jacket sleeve off but I had trouble getting out of my pullover. Caked blood had glued it to my arm. It finally came off but I felt pieces of my skin peeling off with it.

"Ee-yaw!"

I groaned and locked my jaw. It was so NOT fun. I tried running cool water over my arm. Might as well have been hot needles. Then I found another worm and gagged. I flushed the beastie down the sink. Somehow I managed to wash the gouges and puncture wounds, dry them, and daub them with antibiotic cream but I was dancing a jig the whole time. I finally fixed up a bandage of gauze and tape. As I cleared away my mess, I almost tossed my bloody jacket and shirt into the wastebasket. Wah-hoh! Mom would go mental if she found those. I set them on the counter instead.

Then I surveyed my handiwork. Oh, criminy. How was I going to hide those thick bandages? I snapped my fingers. I had a super-large plaid shirt in my closet. The sleeves always dangled to my knuckles. That would work.

Now I had to dispose of the evidence: one ripped-to-shreds bloody jacket plus one blood-stained shirt with the left sleeve hanging by threads. I crept down the stairs with said items tucked behind me checking to make sure I was alone. Grabbing an empty grocery sack, I tossed everything inside, slipped out the back door, and threw the bag into our large dumpster. Only then could I draw in a lung full of air. I must have been holding my breath. My hands were so clammy I had to rub them on my jeans. But, tossing my hair out of my eyes, I cracked my knuckles and strolled back inside.

Man, I need a breather—big time.

As I sat down to dinner, I crossed my fingers. I knew my mother believed in pleasant conversation at meal times but, when dinner went off without a hitch, I had to pinch myself. I mean, I kept my sore arm with the puffy sleeve below the table, asked for the salt and pepper, and plied Mom with questions about her day. She rambled on about all the challenges of her job—she's the new network manager at a local bank—and I pretended to give her my undivided attention.

Don't forget to compliment her on her cooking.

"You make the best roast beef dinner, Mom," I said. She smiled and pushed more potatoes and gravy in my direction. I grinned. *Oh yeah. Way ta go, Barry Boy. Tapped into her motherly heart with that one, didn't ya?* Maybe, just maybe, I had softened her mood for the evening.

However, when the conversation lagged, something struck me as odd. It was Jenny. She hadn't spoken two words the whole meal. *Weird. Jenny usually talks the hind legs off an elephant.*

Even Mom noticed. "Jenny, you've been so quiet tonight. Are you feeling okay?" She put a hand on my sister's forehead.

Jenny shrugged. "Yeah, I'm okay," she said. "Just had a big 'put down' today by somebody I thought was a friend. He had his reasons, I suppose." Then she gave me a sober look. At first I nearly lost it. *She knows about me!* Then I heaved a deep breath and smirked to myself. *Nah. When Jenny knows anything juicy about me, she always blabs it the minute Mom walks in the door.*

But I had to admit that something about my little sister was out of whack. I decided to keep an eye on her. I started making covert sweeps around the table. It was during one of those sweeps that a bell went off in my head. *Whoa. What's this? Jenny's not sitting in her regular seat? Okay, that's crazy. She's always totally Looney Tunes about getting "her" seat.*

After dinner, I got even more shook up when Jenny kept avoiding me. I decided to grab the cat by the tail and get the whole matter out in the open.

"So Jen. How was your day?"

She didn't answer.

Get this. I *knew* she heard me. I mean, she turned and looked me full in the face. But instead of saying anything, she made a beeline for the bathroom.

"Well, fine!" I hissed out in the hall. "Who needs to talk to you anyway?" I stomped off. *Girls are such dingbats.*

As luck would have it, just as the dinner dishes were cleared away, Mom got a call from her bank. The network servers had crashed. She would have to go down and see what the problem was. I tugged at the bandages on my arm and heaved a sigh of relief.

Just then, Jenny walked sober-faced into the kitchen. Dang. What was with her? She was always staring at me. I felt more uptight than a Doberman on a choke chain. Did she know about my arm? I pulled up short. *Yo, Barry, cool it.*

I headed for my room and shut the door determined to stay there all night. But soon I was ready to rip the book shelves off the walls. At last, I swung my door open, and headed downstairs. Jenny sat on the couch, her eyes following my every move. *She's even watching me get a glass of water. Creepy.* Just what was she looking at, anyway? Did I have something painted on my forehead?

Once after raiding the refrigerator for an apple, I rounded a corner and ran smack into her. As her head thumped my chest, Jenny looked up at me in surprise. For a moment, I thought I saw a blue curtain shimmering behind her. Then it was gone.

But it was her face that had me riveted. Her eyes flew open and her hand went to her mouth.

"Ah-h-h! Ah-h-h!" she screamed hopping from one foot to the next. Then she dashed for her bedroom and slammed the door behind her. I heard a *snick*. Jenny had locked herself in her room.

My jaw slid to the floor. No duh. I have never—repeat, never—heard my sister scream. Jenny, afraid? No bleepin' way! This girl didn't have a fear bone in her body. I mean, this was the school mini-Amazon who owned a pet snake and a tarantula, for cryin' out loud.

Okay, so this was where my day caught up with me. What with thinking I saw my dad, maggots, monsters with nasty tails, and a sister freaking out . . . yeah. I went into a tailspin. I raced to my room, slumped down at the edge of my bed, and dropped my face into my hands.

I couldn't figure anything out. All evening my little sister had been as silent as a sphinx. So what made her flip out all of a sudden? Jenny, the original motor mouth, was acting so "un-Jenny" like. I raked my hands through my hair and flopped back on my bed. *So Jen, what gives? Why the big clam-up tonight? Why the screaming she-devil act?*

Then I had a thought. What if there was a maggot on the back of my head?

I ran to the bathroom. Using Mom's hand mirror I checked the back of my head. Nothing. What could be my sister's motive for acting so weird? Did she want to get me in trouble? It wouldn't be the first time. *So is this your new tack, Jen? You think if you make me look bad Mom will come to the "rescue" and chew me out?* Mom! I made a face. Sure glad she wasn't home to see this.

I went to bed, but sleep was a joke. The pain in my arm was intense. Whenever I needed to roll over, I had to wake myself up so I could shift my arm around.

CHAPTER 4: BACKYARD BOMBSHELL

*Anger is a flaming spear seized out of the furnace
with bare hands.
The one who throws it always suffers the worst burn.*
                                             ~Martin Moonglow

Why do I feel so cold? Sheets of water pelt my back and I shiver. I'm again standing on a riverbank, my waders sinking into the gritty mud, watching the river rage in front of me. Driven by the heavy rain, waves toss white froth into the wind. Dozens of men in boots and ponchos slog in the muck around me, but I don't move.

Then, a shout comes from out on the water. A diver breaks the surface, waves his arms and hollers, "I found it!"

A engine roars to life right behind me. I jump and duck just in time as a massive hook swoops right overhead. It is so close I feel the whoosh of air. A crane with a tall boom swings it out over the river. The diver lunges for the hook, grabs it, and disappears into the swirling waves. Then, seconds later, he reappears and gestures a thumbs-up to the crane operator.

I hear the grating sound of metal grinding against metal coming from below the surface of the river. Gradually, the crane hoists a large object out of the water. Mud and debris ooze from every crack. I see the outline of a full-sized van and I feel my gut stiffen. My throat closes up. The van. It's my father's SUV!

I scream, "Dad! Dad, no!"—and race for the edge of the water. Shouting and shoving everyone aside, I plunge into the murky river. The water closes heavy and cold over my head. I hold my breath and claw against the powerful current. Time and again, I see my father's face drift in front of me. I reach out to grab him, but the river is too strong. The more I struggle, the more the current fights me. My lungs ache for air.

"Barry!"

"Ah-h-h!" I gasped—and sat up in bed.

Blast it all! Can't a guy get any sleep around here even on a Saturday?

Then I remembered. Oh, yeah. Gramps' birthday. Mom was throwing a big party for him today and I forgot to set my alarm. Okay, Mom has had this big party for Grandpa planned for months. And, yes, she did remind me of it yesterday and I totally let it slip. So much for my Saturday snooze-in. Now if that had been Dad's voice and we were going hunting today . . . . I shoved that memory way back into my mental "nothing" box.

Then I tried to sit up. The pain in my arm made me catch my breath and I groaned.

Man, I need a doctor.

"Barry!" There she is again. My mom loves to yell outside my door. "We need to load the car so we can get over to Grandpa's and go set up for his birthday party." She turned the doorknob and poked her head into my room. "Oh, good. You're awake. You need to get a move on." She paused. "I'll have breakfast on the table in a few minutes. Can you be ready soon? I'll need some help carrying the big cooler out to the car."

Mr. "Help." Yup. That's my middle name. Ugh. This day is already too long.

Dad never yelled at me. He always opened the door with a quiet, "G'mornin' son. Wanna go for a run today or hit the weights for a half hour? Your choice." How I miss him. I swallowed hard.

Okay, a morning person I'm not. But with Mom, there's no point in arguing. I hauled myself out of bed, shuffled to the bathroom, and stared into the mirror. I saw a skinny kid with grocery sacks under his eyes and a crop of rusted spikes on his head. *Stupid hair.* And my face. It looked like I'd been dragged across a

18

chain link fence. If I slept last night, I sure don't remember it. I tried splashing cold water on my face. It didn't work. I wandered back to my room and dropped, head first, onto my bed like a bag of cement. Ouch! Forgot about my arm.

I rolled over and fumbled around in the closest drawer next to my bed hoping something easy would fall out. I grabbed a pair of jeans. Swinging my legs out I began the chore of pulling them on. My arm was so stiff that, by the time I was done, I was in a cold sweat. But get this: When I tried to stand, the floor came up and whopped me in the face.

Mom knocked on my door. "You okay in there?"

I peeled my cheek off the tiles. "Yeah." I mumbled, wheezing.

"Hurry along. Breakfast is just about ready."

Now getting up off the floor with only one good arm takes coordination, which, as you know, is not my strong suit.

"Coming," I muttered.

The short trip to the kitchen table wiped me out. I slumped down in the nearest chair and cradled my head in my arms.

"Another bad night?" Mom asked.

"Mm-uh," I mumbled.

"Same dream again?" asked Mom.

I tried to lift my head but it was too heavy. "I just wish it would go away, Mom. I am so fried."

"I know, dear. The counselor did warn us; it's just part of the grieving process."

Then I couldn't help it. I bawled like a baby. "I should have tried to save him, Mom," I sobbed. "I'm such a coward."

My mom sighed and placed her arm around my shoulders. "Barry, don't do this to yourself. There were dozens of grown men that refused to go near the flooded river that night."

I snuffled and said, "But, Mom, how come they never found his body?"

Mom knelt beside me. "Son, look at me," she said. "We've been over this before. Think about it. It's been six months without any sign of him. We have to face facts and get on with our lives."

Gee, Mom, you are so tough. But when she moved back to her stove, I heard her sniff and catch her breath.

Jenny appeared and slipped into a chair next to me. I turned my back to wipe my face. *Bet my eyes are still red.* But she didn't look at me. She didn't say one word either. She just poured herself some cereal, gobbled it down in three minutes, and left.

So, what am I now? Chopped liver?

By this time, Mom was headed for the car so I knew I'd better grab a bagel and follow. She had already loaded everything. Oops. Sorry Mom.

I opened the car door. Rats. Mom had put the ice chest in the front seat. Looked like I was sharing the back seat with the Ice Princess. Oo-oo-kay-y-y. Here goes nuthin'.

"Mornin' Jen," I said. Jenny didn't answer. I couldn't help noticing that, the moment I slid onto the seat next to her, she sucked in her breath. Then she scooted over to the far side of the car.

Hey, Snoot Face, why don't you just hug and kiss that door while you're at it? Crud. Why does she treat me like dog barf? Last night her eyes drilled holes in my back. Today she won't even look me in the eye. And I still get the silent treatment.

Not for the first time did it occur to me that Jenny knew something. But what? How could she possibly know about . . . ? Naw.

I sighed, settled my sore left arm in a safe nook on the door, and forced myself to watch the cars on the freeway. For a Saturday morning, the traffic reminded me of a scene out of "It's a Mad, Mad, Mad, Mad World." Drivers raced from stoplight to stoplight, careening across lanes, and cutting in front of anyone they pleased.

The psych ward must be missing a few loonies today, I thought.

Without warning, Mom swerved to avoid a sideswipe.

"Look out!" she warned.

The awkward pitch sent Jenny sprawling onto my leg in spite of her seat belt. She groaned and straightened up. As she did, she glanced up at my face. All of a sudden, she stiffened and sucked in her breath. Again, I saw a curtain of blue around her and her eyes showed total panic. Gasping, she said, "Something . . . is very . . . wrong with you, Barry."

Oh, like duh-h-h . . . .

"What do you mean?" I snapped. "I feel fine."

Jenny shook her head, still staring wild-eyed at me. *How strange. Her face is pasty white.* She made to touch me again, but snatched her hand back. Then she reached out and, this time, planted her hand firmly on my knee.

I heard her squeal. I glanced up front to see how Mom was taking the racket but she had the radio on. Good thing.

I bit my lip. Jenny was so ticking me off. I wondered if she really *was* trying to get me in trouble.

I blew it off. "C'mon, get a grip!" I scoffed. "This is just an act. You're making me out to be some kind of creep."

"Wait," said Jenny. She rifled through her little purse and pulled out a pocket mirror. "Watch what happens when I touch you," she whispered.

Okay. So I held the mirror in front of me while my twerpy little sister placed her hand back on my leg.

What I saw in the mirror knocked the air out of me.

My head! No way! I'm a giant tomato. My eyes are little black dots and my mouth—it looks like a . . . a trout.

When Jenny lifted her hand off my arm my face returned to normal.

That did it. I couldn't help it. I flew into a full blown rage.

"It's just one of your tricks!" I hissed through clenched teeth. I tossed the little mirror back at her just in time to see her chin snap up. At the next stoplight, I saw Jenny's eyes narrow and . . . *oh no! She's poking Mom! Great. Now I'm toast.*

"Hey, Mom!" Jenny said with a nervous little snigger. "Turn around. Watch this."

Traitor. At that moment I could have cheerfully throttled one bratty little sister. I wanted to melt into the seat.

Jenny reached over and slapped her hand down on my kneecap.

"See it, Mom? Can you see it?" Jenny said, her voice squeaking.

Mom checked me out in the rearview mirror, and then looked over at Jenny. "I guess I don't know what you're talking about, dear. What is it I'm supposed to see?"

Jenny's face was priceless. "You don't see anything weird about the way Barry looks?" she asked.

Mom adjusted her rearview mirror to get a better look. I felt like a monkey in a zoo.

"No," she said. "Nothing that a good haircut wouldn't take care of, that is." She turned herself back around and started the car forward. Glancing back at Jenny, Mom said, "Sweetheart, you know I've spoken to you before about annoying Barry. I want you to put your hands in your lap, and keep them there for the rest of this trip. Do you hear me?"

"Yes, ma'am," said Jenny.

I snorted. Then I put my thumbs in my ears, wiggled my fingers, and crossed my eyes. I gave her my snarky head wobble. *Serves you right, you little dweeb. Your tattling backfired. What a hoot!*

Okay, so I had to admit the obvious. Jenny *was* seeing weird stuff and I was too. I watched her turn toward the window, tuck in her chin, and tighten her lips so they almost disappeared between her teeth. But when I saw a large tear roll down Jenny's cheek, my eyeballs nearly fell out of my head. Not possible. My little sister—crying?

Again, when I remembered all the strange happenings of the last twenty hours, I broke out in an icy sweat. *Oh, Dad, if only you were here to talk to, to help me make sense of all this. How could you leave me when I needed you the most?* Again, I choked back my own tears.

Everyone thought the birthday bash for Gramps was a big success—everyone except Jenny and I, that is. One would have thought the other had a disease the way we avoided each other all day. Jenny, as somber as the Grim Reaper, did not speak a word, but watched my every move. If I went out on the deck, she spied on me from a nearby window. If I went for a stroll around the backyard, she crept up behind me.

"I feel like I'm under FBI surveillance," I muttered and heaved a deep sigh. I could be the main character in Zombieland. The thought set my teeth on the edge. And how come Jenny knew something was wrong but Mom didn't?

Then a terrifying thought hit me. *My monster head!* I stopped on the path, a fierce foreboding stabbing me like a ninja dagger. The lizard tail! What if . . . what if that lizard tail had infected me with a terrible disease? Criminy! What if I was mutating into one of those awful ghouls like the one at the arcade? I was a dead man walking. I really could be contagious!

If only I had stayed away from Carl Lumpskin none of this would have happened. Note to self: In the future, give monster-infected bullies a wide berth.

I had to find someplace to hide. *Mom's gonna kill me for leavin' Gramps' party but I've got to get out of here. What if everyone at the party got sick? I need a place to think—somewhere away from Jenny's snooping.* All of a sudden, I felt sick and for the second time in two days, I threw up.

Then I was really wiped. I found a bed of moss behind some large shrubs in my grandfather's backyard. Taking care not to bump my injured arm, I stretched myself out on the moss. My brain felt like a grilled cheeseburger. A light breeze ruffled the trees above my head. Brilliant autumn reds, oranges, and yellows caught the rays of the warm sun. It was a gorgeous Indian summer day. I closed my eyes. Ah, finally. Peace. I hadn't felt this relaxed since . . . . As I dozed off, I had the distinct feeling that I was floating.

All of a sudden, a loud voice right above me chuckled, "Well, there you are! Welcome back, Master Barrington."

I sat up with a jolt!

"What's this . . .?"

I looked around. All I could see was blinding white. Almost afraid to breathe, I lifted my head.

"Oh no. Not again . . . !"

Gazing down at me were two of the most gigantic baby blues I had ever seen.

CHAPTER 5: GIANT!

"There will always be someone more powerful than you. The secret is to beseech the protection of one who is not only powerful but also good.   ~Martin Moonglow

I scrubbed my eyes. I didn't think anything else could surprise me considering all I'd been through lately, but this—this was off the charts. Now I was sure I had one foot on a banana peel and the other in the slime of insanity.

The large eyes belonged to a very large face. The large face belonged to . . . wait. There was something warm under my hands. I gulped. Using my fingers I tested what it was I was sitting on. It felt familiar. Then I looked down.

"Ah-h-h! Skin! I'm sitting on skin!" Whirling around, I slammed into a massive thumb and fingers. "A hand! I'm sitting on a humongous hand!" Scooting back against the fingers, I looked up at the large features hovering over me and gasped.

The giant's skin glowed almost white, and his clothes seemed to be dotted with millions of diamonds. His hair, like snow caught in a blizzard, billowed around his face and into his eyes. And those eyes. Blue as a summer sky. And they had to be the size of turkey platters.

I peered over the edge of the hand and swallowed hard. My grandfather's neighborhood was now nothing but toy houses surrounded by tiny trees swaying in the breeze. The sight made me woozy.

"Criminy! I must be up a hundred feet," I muttered to myself. The giant roared again.

"Aha!" he shouted.

"Ee-yi-ee!" I slapped my hands over my ears. The giant's bellow was like a heavy metal band at full volume.

"I thought you were lost for good!" the behemoth blasted. "I am so delighted to see you again, young man. Yes, indeed!" Then to my shock, the creature began to close up his hand—with me in it!

"No!" I yelled. I dove for the closest finger and pinched it with all my might. The giant let out a loud grunt and opened his hand again.

"A bit cheeky today, I see," he said, clucking at me, his voice softer now. "After your disappearing act this last two weeks, I guess I should not be surprised at your impudence." Again I felt the massive hand closing around me.

"No! Wait!" I shouted.

This time the creature relaxed his fingers more slowly. I saw the giant blink and a quizzical look spread across his face. I sat stock-still. The giant brought his palm up close to his face. Now I was only a few feet from one enormous nostril.

Yo. I can see nose hairs half way up to your brain, big guy.

Using my last ounce of nerve, I yelled, "Stop! Who . . . who *are* you and . . . and what do you want with me?"

The giant frowned and went very still. Then he smiled. Cocking his head to one side, he whispered—even his whispers were loud—" If I didn't know better, I'd think you were trying to talk to me, Master Barry."

At that, I jumped up and stomped my foot.

"I *am* talking to you, you big lummox!" I shouted.

Then I lost my balance.

"Wa-a-hoh!" I howled. I grabbed for the closest finger and latched onto it with all my might. Then, over my shoulder I hollered, "Tell me who you are. And how is it you know my name?"

The giant froze and studied me in silence for a full minute. Then, without a word, he began to stretch skyward until his shoulders just went poof! into the clouds above.

I blinked. Great. Not only has Godzilla trapped me a hundred feet above ground but now he goes headless on me. Maybe my question scared him. I shook my fist toward the sky and shouted, "You come back here and talk to me!"

Out of nowhere, lightning flashed and thunder rumbled. Then I heard the sound of a fierce wind. Now, I don't know if I told you, but I'm a home-grown Missouri boy. I knew what that sound was.

"Tornado!" I screamed and flung myself flat on the great hand. "I'm going to be blown to bits."

I caught hold of a large finger and covered my head with my arms, waiting for the blast of high winds and rain. Nothing happened. The sound grew louder. In fact, it rumbled like a freight train overhead. But there was no wind or rain, just thunder, lightning, and that terrific roar.

Okay, that was when I knew I was cracking up. I was seeing weird things. I was hearing weird things. And now my nightmares were showing up in broad daylight. I had to face it. I was a total nut case. Might as well throw in the towel.

I curled up in a tight ball. *Check out time.*

CHAPTER 6: THE MISSION

*"Sometimes answers create even more questions.
We must accept the fact that we will never know everything."*
          ~Martin Moonglow

  Meanwhile, the giant had embarked on a quest. "Oh Great One! I would have an audience with you!"
  Silence.
  In a more humble tone, the giant called out again, "Oh Honorable Majesty, I need to speak with you."
  A booming voice shattered the quiet afternoon. "Here I am, Martin! What brings you here today? You sound upset."
  "Thank you for granting me an audience, Your Excellency," said the giant. Then he came right to the point. "I have a strange puzzle for you. First, my charge, Master Barrington Klutzenheimer, goes missing for two weeks. Then, today, when I find him, he acts like he can see me."
  More silence. Then the Voice spoke. "No doubt it's because he *can* see you, Martin."
  There was a pregnant pause.

"What!" the giant exploded. Then he began to sputter. "Master Barrington can . . . he can. . . he can see me? How is this?"

"Martin, it just is. That is all," said the Voice.

"But Your Grace, we keepers have remained anonymous for hundreds of millennia. Hasn't this always been your supreme command? I do not understand, Sire."

"No, I'm sure you don't, Martin."

"May I ask the reason for this sudden policy departure, Oh Great Lord?"

"No, you may not."

"But . . . but, Master!"

"Martin, I made the law. I can also break it," the Voice said.

The giant was now beside himself. "But Your Majesty, in all of history, has there ever been an earthling that could see his keeper?"

"Yes, a few times, Martin."

"But why my little Barry, Your Grace? He is just a child. What use could he have of spirit sight?"

"Now, Martin, you know I keep my own counsel. I have my reasons," the Voice answered.

"But . . . but, my Lord! How am I to talk to the boy?" The giant was flustered now. "I haven't used a human tongue for centuries."

"Think, Martin. You've already been talking to him, right?"

"But, Your Grace, surely you can see that I am just not equipped to carry on a conversation with this boy . . . !"

The Voice grew stern. "Martin, are you saying that I don't know what I'm doing?"

"Oh, no, no, Your Majesty," said Martin, forcing his voice to sound more humble. "Far be it from me to question your judgment."

"Seems to me that is exactly what you are doing."

"Please, your Lordship, I am just profoundly surprised. I mean no disrespect."

The Voice answered, "Well, Martin, I'm glad to hear that, at least. Now you just do your job and leave me to do mine."

"But . . . but . . . O Great One, would you consider granting me the Silver Tongue so my speech is clear to the lad?" Martin begged.

"No. That won't be necessary, Martin."

"But, my Lord . . . !"

"Martin . . . !" The Voice was once again very firm. "Must I again remind you that I know what I'm doing?"

"No, Great One. I know you are always in charge," said Martin, chewing his lip. "I accept your direction. Thank you for your confidence in me."

Then the Voice boomed in laughter. "Oh Martin, if you could just see your face right now. Of course, I have confidence in you! Long before this child was conceived thirteen years ago, I chose you to be his keeper. Do you remember that? Do you not know that I picked you and only you for this very mission?"

Martin blinked. There was a mission? "I did not know that, Sire." As the information sank in, Martin bowed low. "I humbly submit to your infinite wisdom. You are way ahead of me as always."

"Thank you. Nice to hear a vote of confidence for a change." The Voice had a hint of a chuckle. Then it continued. "By the way, Martin, just so you know, the boy is not the only one that has been given spirit sight. There is another. You will know who it is in due time."

Martin then pressed for more information. "Great Master, could I ask one or two more questions?"

"And what would those be, Martin?"

"First, does Master Barry understand me? Does he understand Sky Talk? And second, what am I to tell the boy about this arrangement?" the keeper asked.

The Voice was quiet for a moment, and then replied, "The boy does indeed understand every word. I have already seen to that. As for your second question, Martin, you will know what to say to him when the time is right."

Then the azure sky was quiet once more.

I felt the giant move. *Uh-oh. He's back. Now I'm dead meat.*

I looked up and saw the giant's upper torso reappear and I braced myself for the worst. All of a sudden, the hand I was laying on tipped sideways. Like a grub, I rolled off and landed on his other hand. While I was still dizzy, the second hand tilted and the giant dumped me back on his first hand again.

"Would you quit that!" I hollered. "I'm not an insect, ya know."

That's when the giant pulled me up to his face for a second time. *Hey, Glow Man, do you know that the whiskers on your face look like foot-long toothpicks?* Then the giant broke into a grin. He snagged me around my waist with two fingers, lifted me high into the air, and let loose with a massive roar.

"So! Master Barrington Arthur Klutenheimer!" he bellowed.

Remember I told you that the giant's voice was like a thunderclap. No joke. It was so loud I nearly passed out. Then things got worse. The giant lost his grip on me and I dropped like a rock. I fell so fast that I could hear the wind whistling past my ears. The houses below rushed toward me at a frightening speed.

"He-e-elp!" I screamed.

Just as I was about to smash into a tree branch . . . *oof!* I felt the giant's hand snatch me out of thin air.

Chapter 7: Keeper

*"If someone insists on clinging to the old ways,
he trumpets his fear of the new.*
~Martin Moonglow

  I was sure my bones had turned to mush especially when a large finger shoved me toward the hollow of the huge hand. I grabbed my wobbly knees afraid they would slide out from under me. The giant then flicked me around this way and that. I felt like one of the roly-poly insects I often toyed with in my back yard. *Now I'm the bleepin' roly-poly.*

  Aside from his big outburst, the giant had not said a word. At last I could not contain myself and I said, "Are . . . are you going to eat me?"

  Is that my voice? I sound like a duck with laryngitis.

  The giant blinked and grinned.

  "Eat you!" he shouted and started to snicker. That bugged me. Then to add insult to injury, he threw his head forward and doubled over laughing.

  When he did that, he tossed me right back up into the air again. But I hollered and he caught me for a second time. I landed with my head stuck between two thick fingers.

  All this time the giant was still laughing, spinning and charging around like a wild bull at a rodeo. I wrapped my arms around the two fingers with a white-knuckled grip born of sheer terror. Jostled and tipped every which way, first dangling like a noodle from a fork, then tossed like stir-fry in a wok. I had no way of knowing which way was up or down.

Whoozers! Carnival rides have nothing on a rampaging giant. One more minute of this and I'm gonna puke my Nikes.

The giant's roar was so loud I was sure my ears would bleed. But the creature soon calmed down and I felt myself being lifted up again. Positioned right there in front of his face, I could see he was still sniggering and gasping for breath. Huge tears of laughter spilled from his eyes.

Glad you found that funny, you brute. I considered my question quite logical.

"Master Barry," the giant began, "Why *(wheeze)* . . . why would I wish to eat you—you . . . *(snort)* you itty bitty bag o' bones?" He started to laugh again.

"You're not going to eat me?" I asked.

The giant shook his head. "No."

"Why?" I shouted, hoping I sounded gutsy. "Not enough meat for you, is that it?"

Again, the giant started giggling again. "You must forgive me, Master Barry. I have not laughed this hard in eons," he said. "But no, I do *not* wish to eat you. Is that clear enough?"

"W. . .w. . .well, if you're not going to eat me, wh . . . what do you want me for?" I stammered.

"Well, now," said the giant, his face growing quite serious. *"That* is the big question, isn't it?" Then he whispered, still out of breath, "Barry, my dear lad, the answer to your question is—I don't know. That's the truth. This is all very new to me, too. You, me, we are in—how is it that you earthlings say it—unchartered territory?"

Duh. Just pickin' up on that one are you, Sherlock?

Then I got to my feet and put my hands on my hips. "Okay," I hollered, "Just so I'm clear about this, what kind of creature are you? Where did you come from? And why can't you tell me what this is all about?"

"Whoa! Settle yourself, boy. So many questions!" the giant bellowed again.

I dropped to my knees, my hands over my ears. "Do you have to talk so loud?" I said. "You're giving me a migraine."

The giant was silent for a moment. Then, in a loud whisper he said, "In answer to your first question, Barry, I am one of the Sky People, and I live in this world right along with you. My name is Martin and I've known you all your life. Now tell me the truth. Did you really think I would eat you?"

I nodded.

Martin's shoulders jiggled and heaved. "Master Barrington," he said, "I have been right beside you for thirteen years. Not once in all that time have I harmed a single hair on your head. I don't plan to start now."

Okay, that's a bunch of barf in a bag. But then again, he says he's never hurt me even once in . . . wait a minute.

I cleared my throat and said, "Never hurt me, you say. What would you call flying kiteless a hundred feet in the air? A stroll in the park?" I saw Martin blink.

Then a new thought hit me. "Hold on," I said. "Did you say you've been with me for . . . for thirteen years?"

The giant nodded. "That is correct, Barry."

"Ah-ha!" I shouted. "I knew you were a fake. I'm only twelve." I gave my head a wig-wag.

Martin was quick. "From your birth, yes," he said, "but I was including the nine months before you were hatched," said Martin.

"Hatched? You mean 'born', don't you? I'm not a chicken, you know."

"Born, hatched – aren't they the same?" Martin asked. I shook my head. *Not. Hoo-boy. Weird and weirder.*

Out loud I asked, "So why have you been hangin' around me for twelve. . . uh, thirteen years, and how come I'm just now seeing you?"

The giant sighed and answered, "I'll begin with your first question. Let's just say that before you were even a gleam in your father's eye, Master Barry, I was given the privilege of being your keeper."

I slumped down and scooted back against a finger. "Ok-a-ay-y. So-o-o . . . what's a keeper?" I asked.

The giant thought for a moment. "A keeper, a keeper . . . . Let me see." Then he brightened. "A keeper is a Sky Person that watches over an earthling and keeps bad things from happening to him."

I stared into the glowing features. I had to admit that the guy did have a kind face, but . . . *oh, my brain is so whacked. Why can't I be just a regular kid?*

Dragging myself back to the present, I said, "All right. If what you say is true, how come I've never seen you before?" I asked.

The giant shrugged. "I don't know yet. By royal decree we keepers have always remained invisible. But in your case and for some unknown reason, that decree was just rescinded for you and me. The truth is, I was as surprised as you when you started shouting at me. I have never known a charge that could see his keeper. Now, here you are. Not only can you see me but you can also hear me. There's no doubt about it. You have spirit sight."

I groaned and dropped my head between my knees. Then, I jumped up. Pointing my finger at the giant's nose, I spluttered, "Do you have any idea what I've been through these last two days? I've been attacked by monsters, seen maggots crawling out of a guy's mouth, turned into a dorky tomato-head by my sister, and tossed like a salad into the air by a humongous giant." I grabbed my hair with both hands. "It's been scary, I tell ya. I'm freakin' out. I'm two chocolate chips short of a cookie."

Looking up at the giant, I was surprised at the softness in his eyes. He spoke in a quiet voice. "Poor lad," he said, "I wish I had more answers for you."

I collapsed like a tower of Lego blocks and just laid there in Martin's hand rocking back and forth.

"I am *so scared*. My dad's dead. And I can't talk to my mom or my sister. Even my best friend is off in Hawaii. Overnight, everything I've ever known has been flipped upside down and I've been left all alone to figure it out. With my luck, you'll leave too."

The giant drew himself up, indignation written all over his face. "Barrington Arthur Klutzenheimer! I've been at your side for thirteen years. You are my charge. I can never leave you."

I blinked. "You've been with me all this time? Even though I couldn't see you?"

"Yes," said the giant. "Even though you couldn't see me. You are my responsibility and I am very serious about it. When you disappeared, I . . . uh . . ."

I snapped my head up. "What ? Hey, wait," I said. "First you say you can never leave me, and then you say you lost me. Which is it?"

"Well, that's actually correct, Master Barry, and it troubles me to no end," said Martin. "Can you tell me your whereabouts these last two weeks?"

Ah-ha! This guy is bluffing. He doesn't really know who I am or where I've been. He's just stringing me along. I'm not telling this monster diddly-squat.

I felt a hot wave rush up my neck and into my face. "Uh-h. Can't think that I was . . . anywhere unusual," I said trying to act cool. Just then, I felt a stabbing pain in my arm and I winced. *Wonder what this giant would say if I told him about the devil at the arcade.*

It was time to change the subject.

"So, uh," I began, "You say you don't know why I have this spirit stuff?"

"No, Master Barry, I do not. I suggest we run fast," the giant said.

I blinked and stared up at him. *This guy is making about as much sense as a bowling ball on a pogo stick.*

"Um, have I missed something here?" I asked.

The giant sighed. "What I mean is that we have to be quick to catch up on our history together. I also have to teach you the ways of the Sky." I shook my head.

Martin sighed. "I am sorry Barry, lad, but my earth language is still very rusty." At that, he began to laugh all over again. The blast from the great voice sent me into a huddle with my hands clamped over both ears and my eyes scrunched tight. Seconds later, everything went quiet. I peeked out with squinty eyes. The keeper was frowning. Then his eyebrows flew up.

"I think I know how to solve this little problem," he said.

Setting me down on the lawn, he drew himself up to his full height. Without warning, sparkling colors began whizzing off the huge body until it was totally hidden in a swirling rainbow-colored cloud. Then, out stepped a creature now only the size of a man, dressed in glistening silver.

CHAPTER 8: SPIRIT SIGHT

*"Everyone, human or spirit, has a gift. Choosing
to use it is another matter."*
~Martin Moonglow

I stumbled backward, bumped into a tree, and burned bark all the way to the ground.

"How . . . how'd you do that?" I said, my voice cracking.

The glowing man lifted his head and smiled at me. "Oh, we Sky people can be any size we wish. Big, small, even—and this is my personal favorite—*very* small. I prefer two centimeters. It's the perfect size to hitch a ride on your earlobe. But now, Master Barry, I think we need to talk."

But I just sat there, a prickly sensation crawling across on my scalp. Then I couldn't stop myself. I jumped to my feet and bolted for my grandfather's deck. Halfway across the lawn I smacked into a hand the size of a Chrysler. My arms and legs flailed in empty space. Then I was rolling on the ground in front of the strange man.

"You weren't trying to get away from me, were you, Master Barry?" He looked down at his hand—now normal size—and flexed his fingers. "We have so much history to piece together and I'd like to get started if you don't mind. And to make sure we are uninterrupted by anymore shenanigans like that one, let's have our conversation in a setting that is less distracting." I looked at Martin and made a face. Before I realized what was happening, I felt myself floating up into the air. Martin floated right beside me. I stared at the receding ground and began to feel a bit dizzy. Seconds later, Martin settled me on a branch in one of Grandpa's tallest evergreens.

Right off, my hands were so clammy I lost my grip and fell off the branch. My pants snagged a knot and I found myself dangling thirty feet from the ground. Martin reached down and hauled me up, his eyes crinkling. "You might want to keep your body as still as you can," he said. "Keep your mind focused on our conversation. It will keep you from falling."

I cleared my throat. "Al . . . all right, Martin, the used-to-be giant, we'll talk," I said. "But why the funky accent?"

He smiled. "It's British. I learned my English while I worked in India for two centuries. I speak pretty fair Urdu as well."

My jaw sagged. "Urdu? *Two* centuries!" I blurted out. *Hey, doofus. Close your mouth before you catch flies.*

"Yes," answered the giant. "The language is also called Hindi. Aside from English, it's the most prominent language in India."

"But *two* centuries? You can't be two centuries old," I said. *No way this guy is even fifty years old.*

"Oh, I'm way older than that," said Martin.

"Impossible," I muttered. An odd sensation niggled at my spine. *Think Barry. After all you've been through? All you've seen? Maybe your definition of impossible needs a rework.* I cleared my throat. "You . . . you can't be serious. How old are you, *really*?"

Martin stretched out on the limb, crossed his legs, and put his hands behind his head. "Let's see," he said, scanning the sky, "I was a mere cherub when the earth was drying up right after the Great Flood."

"The Great Flood . . . !" I sat up with a jolt and my pants caught on a branch. I yanked them up.

"Not like Noah's ark and . . . and *that* flood?"

"Yes, that flood. In fact, a grandchild of Noah's, Magog, became my first charge."

I stared at him, stunned. "You *knew* Noah!" I said. "What was he like?"

Martin nodded. "Oh, he was a wonderful man. Very patient. Imagine living on that ark with all those animals." Martin chuckled. "Noah would hang his head out a window even in the driving rain just to get away from the smell. One time he almost drowned."

"Then you have to be thousands of years old!!" I exclaimed. "Sorry. That's too much of a stretch."

"Believe what you want," said Martin with a shrug. "I'm—how do you humans put it?—'more aged than rocks.'"

"'Older than dirt' is what we say," I said. I shifted my weight. My rump had gone numb sitting on that hard branch. "All's I can say is that this is off-the-charts spooky. You show up out of nowhere, yet you say you've been here all along. I just don't get it. How come I'm just now seeing you?"

"I told you. You have spirit sight, Barry."

I sagged—and nearly fell out of the tree again. "What is spirit sight?" I asked.

"Well . . ." Martin answered. "There are these spirit folks who live in the air. There are good ones and bad ones. The good spirits are charged with protecting humans from the bad spirits. Spirit sight is the gift of being able to see both the spirit world and your world as well. As for the fact that only you can see the spirits, I do not know why that is."

Then Martin got very serious. "Barry, am I the only one you've seen so far?"

I blinked. I had a sudden flash of the spike-tailed monster at the arcade. "Well, not exactly," I said. "I've been seeing some awful weird things."

At that moment, the wind kicked up and my branch bucked like a bronco in a rodeo. I held on so tight my knuckles turned white. Martin's branch was whipping around even worse than mine but he didn't even uncross his legs.

"Um . . . can we go down to the lawn again? My brain gets fuzzy at high altitudes."

Martin grinned. "Sure, Master Barry." He grabbed the back of my jacket and together, we slowly descended to the grass below.

I rubbernecked the whole back yard and sat down. My skin felt all prickly. "Are you saying there are other spirits around here?" I whispered.

Martin nodded and joined me on the ground. "Of course," he said. "Spirits live all around you. Humans who cannot see the spirit world have no idea we exist, but we're here. When we do battle with the evil ones, there can be tremendous upheavals. Earthlings try to explain what they see happening, but with their limited vision, they're usually wrong."

I'm sure my eyes bulged to the size of oranges. "Battles! You mean spirit wars?"

"Of course. Good and evil are always at war. Many fierce creatures live on this planet, young master, and don't you forget it," Martin said, his expression very grave.

I rubbed my arm. "Um . . . what kind of creatures? Do they attack people?"

"Yes, they do. All the time. They attack humans to get at us. During the days I couldn't find you—last week, in fact—I was called up for a nasty skirmish in a town on the other side of those hills. I saw some powerful demon spirits I haven't seen in a hundred years. They were trying to set up a garrison. Evil beings were threatening even the good homes. When the people in the town begged the Prince for protection, the Prince gave us keepers permission to go after them. Those savages will think twice before they try that again. Loathsome creatures they are."

"Wow! A sky battle. Will I ever see one?" I asked.

"I'd say you will not be able to avoid it," said Martin.

"Far out! A sky war! Way cool!"

"No, young master, it is not 'way cool' as you put it. All wars are ugly, but they must be fought. Evil must—*it will*—be defeated. If humans could only see the horror these evil creatures incur, they would never invite them into their lives.

"Wait. Invite? Did I miss something here?" I asked. "Who deliberately opens the door to bad spirits, for cryin' out loud?"

"Oh, humans don't realize what they are doing," said Martin. Then he paused and stared me right in the eyes. His voice was very quiet when he said, "Perhaps the best example is you, young master."

I blinked. "Me?" *Oh, here we go again. The ol' Blame Barry Game.*

Martin nodded. "That's the only explanation for your disappearance."

"And what's that supposed to mean?" I demanded. *Ten minutes into our first meeting and this guy's already on my case.*

"Somehow, you did something that left you wide open to attack," said Martin. "It must have been a powerful demon that got to you. He was able to keep you hidden from me for fifteen days. I looked everywhere."

Uh-oh. I searched Martin's eyes. "You mean . . . you mean you weren't around to protect me for two whole weeks?" I asked.

"That's right, Barry. And to tell you the truth, I was one frantic keeper."

Well, that explains the monster at the arcade. I wonder what he'd say if I told him . . . . I decided it was time. I rolled up my sleeve and removed my bandages. "Maybe that would explain this," I said.

Martin blinked and leaned forward with his jaw clenched. Then he let out a low whistle. "That's a mighty ugly wound, Barry," he said. "Mind describing the kind of creature that did this?"

I shuddered. "It was horrible," I said. "I was at the video arcade and there was this bully that wouldn't get out of my way. When he wouldn't move, I punched him real hard, see? But when I did, he turned into this slimy monster with a raunchy tail that had spikes on it. The tail wrapped itself around my arm and . . ."

"Yes, I can see what it did," said Martin. "You say this creature was here in this town?"

I nodded. Martin took hold of my arm and examined it. "Have you've been washing it and putting salve on it?" he asked.

"Of course," I said in a what-kind-of-dunce-do-you-think-I-am tone of voice. "But it doesn't seem to be doing any good. In fact my whole side feels like a furnace."

"I'm sure it does," said Martin, nodding his head.

That's all he can say? How can he be so smug? Maybe the throbbing in my arm was getting to me but all of a sudden a boiling rage welled up inside me. *I'll bet he's never felt real pain in his whole spirit existence.*

"So, where *were* you?" I demanded. "Why did you let this happen? How come you didn't protect me?" I stood up and stared down at Martin. I wanted to jab my finger into his pompous chest.

"It's a no brainer and you know it," I said. "*You* fell down on the job, didn't you? And you want *me* to take the rap for it? Ha! Nice try." I plopped back down, still fuming.

The keeper was silent for a long while. Then he nodded. "Yes, I would say that's a pretty typical human response."

"Typical human response!" I was ready to burst a blood vessel. "Nothing about my last forty-eight hours has been typical. I don't see anybody else being attacked by monsters. I don't see anybody else running around with chunks gouged out of their bodies. I don't see anybody else being tossed in the air by giants. And you have the gall to imply that this is my fault? Give—me—a—*break!*"

Martin stood up, hands on his hips, and glared down at me.

Uh-oh. Me and my big mouth.

CHAPTER 9: SKY WORLD DO'S AND DON'TS

Most earthlings are oblivious of Sky culture. When their lives crash and burn, they do not know the reason why."
~Martin Moonglow

"Now you listen to me, Master Barry," Martin said. His voice alone told me I was in deep doo-doo. "Just because you don't always *see* the evil doesn't mean that it's not there. Millions of humans walk this planet everyday with life-threatening wounds much worse than yours, and they don't even know it." He glowered down at me. "You have spirit sight. Now you can see—and feel—the damage these monsters do. And yes, the responsibility for that wound is yours, Barry. Not mine."

I swallowed hard. Martin dropped down onto the grass and glared at me.

Finally he sighed. "Barry, lad, don't you see? I simply don't know what happened to you. One minute, I had you tucked safely in my pocket. The next minute . . . you were gone. Just like that. You humans are free to choose whatever company you want."

I jumped up and grabbed at my hair. "Choose? *Choose?* How could I possibly choose the company of . . . of creatures I didn't even know existed!"

"Doesn't seem fair, does it?" said Martin in a totally-too-calm voice.

My legs wimped out and I sagged onto the grass.

"I hate this spirit stuff!" I swabbed a sleeve across my eyes. "Take it away. I don't want it."

"I wish I could help you, Barry, but it's out of my hands," said Martin.

I blinked and jerked my head up. *What the . . . ?*

"You've got power oozing out of your pores!" I spat out. "Don't try to deny it. This should be a piece of cake."

"I'm sorry, Barry," Martin said. "But since I did not give you the spirit sight, it is not my place to take it away."

I groaned and turned away. *Oh, Dad, where do I go from here? My head feels like a cantaloupe on a soccer field. One more kick and my brains will splatter all over the ground. . . . Hey, wait a minute.*

I whirled back. "Hey, are you saying that you *know* the guy who saddled me with this . . . this jinx?"

Martin cocked his head to the side. "I wouldn't call it a jinx, Barry, but yes, I do know this person," Martin said.

"Must be somebody that enjoys driving people bonkers," I muttered.

Martin leaned back against a tree and folded his arms. "Master Barry, let's not be too hasty in calling this gift a bad thing just because you don't understand it yet. Yes, I *do* know the one who gave you spirit sight, and he always gives out good things, never bad."

I slumped forward. "So I suppose you know what it's like to be attacked by multi-headed goblin. And you've had *your* body parts turned into mincemeat, right? And you've been catapulted a hundred feet in the air with no parachute, right?"

"Master Barry, I can only imagine how confusing this is for you," said Martin.

I threw up my hands. "If this spirit sight stuff is *good* in your book, I shake in my shorts to hear what you call bad." I took a deep breath. "So . . . who dumped this on me?"

"The Majesty, of course," said Martin in a tone that I considered far too matter-of-fact.

"The Majesty?" I tossed my head. "Okay. Well, please tell this Majesty guy that I don't want his spirit sight. Ask him to take it away—like now."

"Oh, he already knows, Master Barry," said Martin.

"He does?" I asked. "And in spite of all I've been through, he's not going to take it away? He must be a sadist. He must enjoy bringing pain to people." I wrapped my head in my arms. "Argh-h-h! My brain is mush!"

If this spirit sight stuff just wasn't so bleepin' scary. Oh Dad. Why did you have to leave? I'm so lost without you!

Okay. So I burst into some very unmanly tears.

Martin sat very still while I pulled myself together. Then he said, "Master Barry, perhaps if I told you about The Majesty, we both would feel better."

I scrubbed my nose, sniffed, and muttered, "I doubt it but give it your best shot."

Martin nodded. "I've known The Majesty for my entire existence. He never does anything without a purpose and it's always a *good* purpose. I can assure you that giving you spirit sight is part of a brilliant plan. Not once have I ever seen his plans go . . . how you do say it . . . 'bally-oop'?"

"'Belly-up'," I said. "I still don't get it. Who is this Majesty person?"

This can't be the same guy I learned about in Sunday School. Surely . . . Then, I realized I didn't want to know. I stood up.

"No! Don't tell me," I hollered. "I refuse to be part of this so-called 'brilliant' plan and that's final. Tell the Majesty I want my life back. I'm going home." With that, I took off across Gramps' front lawn, onto the street, and turned toward home.

Out of nowhere, a large truck careened onto the street, and screeched to a halt so suddenly, that it swung sideways and smashed into a parked Lincoln just inches from my chest. For a split second, I was sure I saw Martin in front of me.

I dropped to my knees, dazed. Behind me, I could hear doors banging and people hollering as the whole neighborhood rushed outside to see what had happened. In a matter of seconds, a dozen people surrounded me.

"Kid! Are you okay?" It was the driver of the truck. "Man, you scared me to death! You came out of nowhere!" He knelt down next to me. "Ya know, you nearly bought that one, don' cha, son?"

I tried to answer but I could only nod my head.

"Somebody call 911!" I heard a voice in the crowd say.

That yanked me out of my stupor. I stood up. "No. I'm okay," I said. "I'm fine."

"Are you sure?" the truck driver asked.

"That was a close shave," said an old man that I recognized as one of Grampa's party guests.

I saw my mother then pushing through the crowd. "Barry!" she cried and threw her arms around me. "Son, are you all right? Whatever possessed you to dash out into traffic like that?"

I hugged her, relieved to be alive. "I'm okay, Mom, really. Just a little shaky."

"Check it out!" muttered a kid on the sidewalk. I looked where he was pointing. The Lincoln was nearly ripped in half. Three more inches and I would have been a slab of meat in a metal sandwich.

I saw Martin then, standing on the other side of the street, his arms folded and a sober look on his face.

Mom was talking to me trying to get me inside to lie down but I shook my head. "I need to walk around for a minute." I had to talk to Martin. *I'm sure I saw him in the middle of that crash.*

Mom took me by the shoulders, eyed me closely, and then gave me another huge hug. "Oh Barry. If anything were to happen to you . . . ." From the way her voice caught I knew she was fighting tears.

"I'm not hurt, Mom, really. Don't worry about me, okay? I'll stay close to the house if you need me." I was past caring whether she could see Martin or not.

I pulled myself away and managed to get to the back yard. Out of sight of the crowd, I flopped down under a tree. Martin came and sat down beside me.

For several minutes we both just sat there. I was still coming to terms with the whole-life-flashing-before-me thing. But finally, I had to ask, "So did you rig that car crash?"

Martin was very still. Then he said, "No, I did not, Barry."

It took me a moment to digest that. "You mean, that was just an random accident?" I asked.

"Yes," said Martin. "It was a random accident."

"But how come . . . ?" I whispered.

"These things happen, that's all," Martin said.

All of a sudden, I felt a wave of ice flood my veins. "But I saw you in the *middle* of the crash," I said. "You were standing right in front of that truck."

"That's right, Barry." Again, Martin's answer sounded clipped.

"But why?" I asked. "If you didn't do it, why were you standing right there?"

"Because the Majesty allowed me to protect you," said Martin.

"Oh."

He then added, "If I had not been standing between you and that big vehicle, you would not be sitting here, and we would not be having this conversation."

"All right," I said, "So I'm not the brightest crayon in the box. Big trucks crashing right under my nose? Right. I get it. The Majesty—whoever he is—has given me spirit sight and that's that. If I argue . . .blam!"

Martin looked over at me. Then his eyes crinkled up and he began to laugh. Whether it was the relief of finding myself still alive or the ridiculousness of seeing this strange man rolling around on the ground, I joined him laughing too. In fact, we laughed for the next three minutes.

When I could catch my breath I said, "Guess I should be glad you're here, Martin."

"I'm glad too, dear boy," he said as he wiped his face.

I sat up straight. "Martin, have you asked The Majesty why he gave me this spirit sight?"

"You may not believe this, Master Barry, but I was confused too—I still am—but all he would say is that we would understand when the time was right."

I groaned. "Another two days of this and I'll be a blubbering idiot, a worthless blob. Then what will happen to his big plans?"

Martin hooted. "To listen to you, one would think the whole world was coming to an end."

"Well, hasn't it?" I mumbled. I pulled up a handful of grass and tossed it into the air.

Martin laughed. "I know for certain it has *not*, Master Barry. Buck up, my boy. You and I are standing on the threshold of the greatest adventure of the century. The Majesty has given us an opportunity—a mission, he called it—something that is almost unheard of in Sky circles. All we have to do is reach out and grab it. Let the Majesty take care of the rest. You can trust him. We have everything to gain and nothing to fear!"

"Right. Um . . . I'm afraid of being hit by big trucks. Does that count?"

Martin went on. "And you want to know something?"

"What?" I said.

"I've already discovered that you are a pretty spectacular human, do you know that?"

"Yeah?" I said. I had to smile in spite of myself. "How's that?"

"Brave, gutsy." Martin grinned. "You don't back away from a threat even when you are frightened. You're smart, too. You're picking up on the ways of the sky so quickly that I feel like I have to scramble to keep ahead of you."

"Yeah," I said, "And when I don't learn quick enough, I get the willies scared out of me, is that it?"

I sighed and leaned sat back taking a few seconds to study Martin again. I had to admit that I liked him.

"You're not so bad yourself," I said. *No offense, Dad, but Martin already knows stuff about me that I could never tell you.* "Now that you're not a giant, you look almost normal—except for the shiny threads, of course."

Martin chuckled. "Barry, you are the kick of the pantaloons!" Then he stood up and shook out his sparkling robe. "So, am I to understand that my 'threads,' as you call them, are not *de rigueur*?" He chuckled again.

"Well, since nobody can see you, I guess it's no big deal."

"No big deal," Martin rolled that around on his tongue. "No big deal. Interesting. I like that." He plopped himself back down on the ground. "I suppose I could change my appearance. But as you said, the only one that can see me is you—and, I'd say, your sister over there."

"Jenny?" I looked over my shoulder. "Jenny's here? Where! Oh, pul-leez, not my sister!" I covered my face with my hands. "She's the *last* person I want seeing you!" I leapt to my feet. "Martin, you don't understand. She can't be allowed to see you!"

Martin shrugged. "Barry, your sister has been watching us since I first found you over behind those bushes. Of all the people at this party, she's the only one who has followed everything that has happened. She's back there staring at me right now." With that, he gave a little two-fingered wave toward the bushes. "Yes, she sees me all right. She just ducked her head." Martin brightened. "I'd say she has spirit sight just like you, Master Barry."

I threw myself to the ground. "Martin, you've really gone and done it now!"

Chapter 10: Family Affair

"Whether on earth or Shomara, our choices have simultaneous consequences in both worlds."
~Martin Moonglow

"Master Barry!" Martin stammered. "I assure you I had nothing to do with this. Remember, I am not the one who gives out spirit sight." Martin looked toward the bushes. "Poor thing. She must be very frightened."

"Jenny scared?" I said with a sneer. "That'll be the day. You don't know her. She's spying on me so she can tattle to Mom. Now my goose is cooked for sure!"

Martin blinked. "You prefer eating *raw* goose?" he asked.

"It's just an expression," I mumbled. "It means I'm in big trouble." I picked up a rock and flung it hard at the nearest tree.

Martin shrugged. "Oh, well. You should never count your birdies before they're born."

"That's 'Never count your chickens before they hatch,'" I said. Under my breath I muttered, "Today I'd be better off *being* the chicken."

Martin nodded his head, "Go ahead, Master Barry. Call her over here. I would like to make her acquaintance."

"You have no idea what you're asking," I muttered. With a low groan, I called out to my sister. "Jen, we know you're back there. Might as well come out from behind that tree."

The shrubbery rustled. Then I heard a loud sob. Jenny broke through the bushes and bolted for the house. Shocked, I looked over at Martin.

"Perhaps you should go see what's wrong, Barry," Martin said.

I scrambled to my feet. As I dashed toward the house, I saw Jenny fly around the edge of the deck. I raced after her, taking the corner at a full run.

Whoa! I stopped short. There she was, just a few yards away, leaning against a tree crying like her heart would break.

Right then—okay, I admit it—right then, something melted inside me. I stepped over to her. When I touched her she quivered like a frightened rabbit. I'd never seen her like this.

"Hey, Jen-Jen," I said using my pet name for her. "Sorry you're so scared," I whispered. I touched her shoulder and she leaned into me.

There's that shiny blue stuff around her again.

"You gonna be okay?" I asked and patted her arm.

Jenny cried for another full minute. Then she stopped, stiffened, and lifted her teary eyes up to my face. *Here goes. She's either going to shove me away or . . . .*

I really did not want her to push me away again—and she didn't. With eyes like saucers, she just stood there searching my face.

After a moment, I said, "Tell me what you see, Jen. Do I still look like a big red tomato?"

She shook her head. Then she threw her arms around my neck and broke into another bout of crying. *Okay. This is freaky. This is not the Jenny I know.*

As her snivels subsided, she choked out, "Oh Bar . . . Barry! I am so glad that you're back to n . . . normal. Everything has been so spooky lately. I've been all eaten up ins . . . side."

"Well, I don't know how normal I am yet," I said. "Something really strange is going on. I haven't figured it out yet, myself."

I held Jenny and waited for her to settle down. I even rocked her and she began to relax. *Hoo-boy. It's been a long time since I've hugged my sister. Maybe I've been too hard on her. She must feel just as alone as I do.* I decided that if I was going to have a partner, Jenny would be as good as any.

I cleared my throat. "Jen," I said. She looked up at me.

"Uh, kid . . . ," I said tugging at her hair. "I know everything is pretty weird right now. You and I are the only ones that can see this stuff. But it looks like we're in this together."

Jenny stared at me and shed a few more tears. *This is incredible. My sister has turned into a water hose.* I put my arm around her shoulder. "Hey, where's that Buffy-the-Vampire-Slayer of Chester Elementary School? Come on. I want you to meet somebody."

"Okay," said Jenny. She sniffed and ran her sleeve across her nose.

"Wait," I said, "Don't ruin your outfit. You can wipe your eyes on my shirt-tail." I pulled her chin up. "Just promise you won't blow your nose on it, okay?" Jenny giggled. It sounded good.

When we got to the back yard, Martin rose to his feet.

"Hello there, Miss Jenny," he said. "How are you doing? My name is Martin, and I am Barry's keeper." With that, he reached out, took Jenny's hand and kissed her fingers. For a moment, I thought I saw a full rainbow of colors swirling around them.

"Uh . . . hi."

Oh, too funny. Jenny's mouth flew wide open. I had to bite the inside of my cheeks to keep from snickering. *So, Little Sister, guess you've never had your fingers kissed before. I can also see that you liked it—big time.* Jenny's eyes were bugging out and she was blushing. I had to really stuff the cackle welling up in my throat. *Jenny at loss for words. Oh, this is choice.*

"So, Miss Jenny, are you feeling better? I hope so," Martin said. "Please sit down." Trance-like, she sat down on the lawn not taking her eyes off of Martin. I flopped down beside her.

The keeper studied her for a moment and then said, "Jenny, it seems you have been given spirit sight along with Barry. I'm sure this comes as a tremendous shock. It has for your brother. Perhaps you can begin by telling us what you have seen so far."

"I don't get it," Jenny said, her voice shaky. "What's spirit sight?"

I sat up. "It's like this, Jen," I said. "You and I can now see the spirit world. Martin here is a good spirit and he's been my keeper all my life. But I haven't been able to see him until today.

There are bad spirits too. Martin says it's the keeper's job to protect us from the bad spirits."

"That's right, Master Barry," said Martin. "Now, Jenny, can you tell us what you have seen so far?"

"Well . . ." Jenny began, "I . . . this is all so weird. I saw you when you were that humongous giant, and I saw you throwing Barry around up in the air." Jenny glanced sideways at me and giggled. "You looked so funny, Barry. Positively green."

"Thanks a heap," I said.

Jenny went on. "After that, I saw you—whoever you are—shrink down to . . . to whatever it is you are now. But before all that, the first thing I saw was Barry's awful red monster head. E-e-ew!! It was *so* creepy!"

Jenny slapped her face with her hands then dug fists into her eyes. "It would come out only when I touched him. That's why I've been staying away from you, Barry. I just didn't want to see it anymore. It made me crawl."

"Mom . . ." Jenny's voice quivered again. ". . . Mom couldn't see any of it, and . . . and it's all been so horrible around our house. I couldn't talk to anybody . . . ." Tears spilled from her eyes and she sniffled.

Martin offered her a handkerchief.

"Th-thank you," she said and wiped her cheek. She looked down at the handkerchief. "Wow, this is so soft."

"Jenny," Martin said, "Spirit sight is an amazing gift. You and your brother must be very rare human children. Though I still do not know why this has happened, I know about the Gift Giver. He always has a good reason. To tell you the truth, I'm on needles and tacks to know what that is. Trust me, Jenny. You and Barry are in for an amazing adventure."

Jenny looked over at me and tried to smile. I chuckled. "Jen, you look like a blob of ice cream left out in the sun." She just sniffed.

Martin went on in a quieter tone. "But now, Jenny, can you tell us what happened when you first saw Barry with his swollen red head?"

Jenny thought for a moment then said, "Well, that was later. What I noticed first was this yucky smell when I passed Barry on the stairs. At dinner last night, I couldn't even sit next to him because he stunk so bad."

I sat back, stunned. "Okay. That's a revelation. I smelled bad?"

Then, from the deck behind us, a voice raked the air. I felt my hair stand on end.

"Grams, here they are!" It was Mom.

Jenny's hand flew to her mouth and we both looked over at Martin.

"Don't worry, guys," said Martin. "Your mother cannot see me. Just be your natural selves," he said. Then he winked.

"What's up, Mom?" I called.

"Barry, Jenny. We're about to head back home. Could you two help your grandmother by cleaning up any trash left out here in the yard?"

Mom didn't wait around for an answer, but swung back into the house. I looked at Jenny. When I thought about it later, I knew I should've kept my mouth shut—but hind sight is always 20/20, right?

I proceeded to shoot my mouth off. "I see Mom's actually including *you* in the work this time. I'm just surprised she didn't say,"—and I used my fake "Mom" voice—"'Barry, I want you to do garbage detail. Jenny can come in and help me serve cookies.'"

I knew by the look on Jenny's face that I'd blown it. She looked like a cat hunching its back. I fully expected to see real claws any second.

"For your information, Barry," she hissed, "I help Mom a lot. Just because you don't *see* me do it is no reason to accuse me of dodging my chores around the house!"

All of a sudden, from out of nowhere, fiery objects whizzed over our heads. Then Jenny screamed. In a nanosecond, two massive hands squashed us together.

After a long minute, Martin called out, "You two all right?" In an instant the great hands shrank to normal size and for a second time, I saw Martin flex his fingers.

"I'm okay." Then I looked over at Jenny. "Hey! Jenny's bleeding!"

Martin reached over and pulled Jenny's hand away. A deep gash sliced across Jenny's upper arm. Martin cleared his throat. "Jenny has been injured, Barry."

Like, yeah. I've got eyes, Keeper-man.

"You *do* know this could have been avoided," Martin said.

I looked at him. "What do you mean?" I asked. "We were crammed under your monster hands tighter than sardines."

Martin heaved a sigh. "Not at first, Master Barry," he said.

"Not at . . .?" I started to say. Then I scowled. "Are you telling us that this happened *before* your hands kablooied into giant paws."

"Yes, Barry," Martin said. "The instant I saw the danger, I covered you. But think. What was going on just before that?"

I stared at him. "J-Jenny and I were arguing?" I stammered.

"That's right, Barry," said Martin, "And the demons took full advantage of that little spat and shot your sister with one of their darts."

Oh sure. When all else fails, blame the boy.

"Oh, so this is all my fault?" I asked squaring myself up. I felt Martin's hand on my shoulder.

"Well, yes and no, Barry," said Martin. "It was bound to happen, and I'm almost glad it came about the way it did. It could have been much worse."

"Why do you say it was bound to happen?" I asked.

"Because you children are still unschooled in the ways of the Sky," he said. "Neither of you realizes that, in the spirit world, there are many different evil spirits. They don't hesitate to attack. An argument is like a flashing bull's eye. They love it. Before we keepers can react, they can unload at least one round of arrows. I have seen it thousands of times. Trouble is, people don't know what's happening so they begin fighting with each another. It's so sad."

Whoop-de-doo. Everything gets dumped on me.

"So, this was all my fault?" I muttered.

"No Barry," Martin said. "Both you and your sister played a part in this. But let's not play the blame game here. What's important is that you children use this as a learning experience. If you do, it probably will not happen again."

"But what about Jenny's wound?" I asked.

Martin smiled. "Oh, that's just a small scratch. I can take care of it." He reached over and touched Jenny's arm. The gash closed up and disappeared right before our eyes.

Jenny sucked in her breath. "Aw-w . . . ! Barry! Did you see that!"

"Yeah, I saw it—but I don't believe it," I exclaimed. "Far out, Martin!"

Martin just smiled.

CHAPTER 11: THE SURPRISE GIFT

*"Though we may have different gifts,
they all come from the same Giver."*
~Martin Moonglow

    I cleared my throat. Looking over at Jenny, I said in my best off-hand voice, "So, you said I smelled bad yesterday." Jenny nodded. I shook my head.
    ". . . But I washed before dinner last night," I said. "I even used soap . . . ."
    Jenny shrugged. "I'm just telling you what I smelled," she said. "Don't take it personally."
    I heaved a heavy sigh. "I knew there was somethin' bugging you last night. You were so quiet I thought you had your jaws wired shut. And the way you stared at me. Like you were stabbing me with a knife."
    "Yeah," said Jenny nodding, her curls bouncing up and down like springs. "The minute you came home yesterday, the whole house reeked. It was like . . . like . . . ." She looked me full in the face. "Do you remember the time when we dug up our Cousin Nate's old dead dog? That's what the smell was like. Gross—with a

capital 'G'!" Jenny shuddered then added, "I kept waiting for Mom to say something but she never did and you know Mom's got the best nose in the family. But even when I moved to the other side of the table, you still made me gag."

Jenny turned to Martin. "His scary tomato head didn't show up until later that night. Then I *really* wigged out. But today in the car is when it hit me. I realized nobody else could smell Barry or see that disgusting head except me. I felt so alone. I thought I was headed for the funny farm."

Martin and I just sat there staring at Jenny.

Jenny cocked her head at me. "So how come you're back to normal? I mean you don't stink, and your head doesn't morph anymore."

In my best Dirk Dastardly voice I said, "Don't be too sure, Little Sister. Maybe I deliberately put on my special stink juice just for you. And maybe I invented the big red head to . . . ."

"Oh-h-h!" said Jenny and clunked me on the head with her knuckles.

I rubbed my head and grinned. "We big brothers have a reputation to keep up, ya know. We're *supposed* to scare our sisters." She laughed.

Turning to Martin, I said, "So, how is it that Jenny could smell me and I couldn't?"

Martin shrugged. "Simple Barry. Jenny has a gifted nose. She smells things that others cannot."

"And what about my tomato head? Where'd that come from?" I asked.

Martin pursed his lips. "Master Barry, anytime there is a red manifestation, it's a sign of anger," he said. "So tell me. Have you been angry recently?"

Hooboy. Bingo. I felt very tired all of a sudden. A rush of scenes fast-forwarded through my brain.

"Angry? Yeah. In fact I've been feeling like Chief Raging Bull," I said. "Especially since Dad died. I know he couldn't help dying, but it just makes me mad for some reason. Like, how *dare* he leave us all alone like this?"

I stopped and looked from Martin to Jenny. "And Mom. I don't know how she is with you, Jen, but she seems to be always on my case. Have you noticed how she keeps giving me all the chores that Dad used to do? I'm only twelve, for cryin' out loud. And do I get any thanks? No. The only reward I get for doing one job is to get another one. She can so tick me off."

And school is so boring. And with Chad off to Hawaii and me stuck at school with nobody to hang out with . . . .

Jenny spoke up. "If it's any help, Barry, I've noticed that Mom has been really dumping on you lately. I just didn't know what to say is all."

"Well I'm glad you noticed. And home isn't the only place have I been getting heat. There are these bullies at school, see? Hardly a day goes by that they don't pester me. I guess I just came unglued. So Martin, let me get this straight. Whenever somebody's angry, it's like putting out the welcome mat for bad spirits, is that it?"

"Yes, Master Barry. And believe me, it had to be one powerful demon to hide you from me for two whole weeks."

Jenny looked puzzled. "Ok-kay-y . . ." she said. "I'm confused. I mean, I've been able to see you, Barry."

You just think you see me, Little Sister. You have no clue what's going on in my life.

"It's different in the spirit world, Miss Jenny," Martin said. "If a human gets trapped by a particularly wicked demon, that demon can cloak the person and keep him hidden from all good spirits."

"So this was the first time that you ever lost Barry?" asked Jenny.

"That is correct, Miss Jenny. The truth is, this is the first time I have ever lost a charge in all my years of service. I was one frantic keeper."

"And how long have you been in service, Martin?" asked Jenny.

"Martin is ancient, Jenny," I said. "He knew Noah – you know – the guy that built the ark?"

"No kidding?" She stared at us. *She's finding that tough to wrap her head around just like I did.*

Jenny was silent for a full minute. But to my surprise, she bounced to up on her knees and said, "Well, I'm just happy you don't stink anymore, Barry. My sniffer is happy too." She wrinkled her tiny nose and laughed. *Her giggle is so cute.*

Then Jenny added, "I'm also glad I don't have to have this spirit stuff all to myself. I'd go clean out of my gourd if I couldn't *talk* to somebody about it."

Turning to Martin, she piped, "So, Martin, you're a . . . a . . .

what did you call it . . . a keeper?"

Martin nodded. "Yes, Jenny. The Great One assigned me to Barry here the moment he was conceived. I've been his keeper all his life even when he was growing in the womb. You might say I knew him before your parents did."

I stood up and found a low tree branch to practice my chin-ups.

Just then, Martin rolled over and peered up at me, grinning. "Do you know what a cute little guy you were? Do you know that you sucked your thumb all during the time you were growing inside your momma? And every night you got the hiccups. You kept your mother awake until she was fit to be tied."

I scraped my hand on a piece of bark and dropped to the ground. "Thanks for that little piece of history, Martin," I growled.

Of course, my sister let out a loud whoop and doubled over. "Barry sucked his thumb! Such a pwecious widdo t'ing!"

I tucked my lips in tight. Then I had a thought.

"Martin," I said, "Does everybody have a keeper at the beginning?"

Martin eyebrows flew up. "Of course, Barry."

Jenny stopped laughing. "What? Hey, hold on," she said. "Does that mean I have a keeper too?"

Martin nodded, "Yes, Jenny, you do."

I watched Jenny's eyes get wide. *Wait for it . . . .*

Jenny lifted her little pointed chin and said, "So where is he? Where's my keeper?"

Gotta love it.

Martin's eyes began to dance. "In truth, little Jenny," he said, "your keeper has been here all along. Right now, you are sitting on her big toe."

CHAPTER 12: AMELIA STARFIRE

"A surprise is often like a pregnant cat. One never knows how many kittens will be in the litter let alone what colors will show up."
~Martin Moonglow

Jenny stared at Martin, her face a total blank. Then her eyes dropped to the place where she was sitting. A split second later, she shrieked like a banshee and leapt to her feet. There, planted in the center of the lawn, was a huge glowing foot, right where she had been sitting. Jen was so flustered that she lost her balance and stumbled backward onto the grass. Stock-still, there she lay, her eyes riveted on what towered above her.

The creature was magnificent. Dressed in a long, sparkling robe of iridescent aqua the same shade as a tropical sea, the giant appeared to be female.

Oh, duh. The blue glow. I was seeing Jenny's keeper all this time.

Her long hair rippled out behind her glowed like gold threads in the sun. Though gigantic, every move she made took my breath away.

Wow. What a stunner. She's as tall as Martin was—that is, before he did the old shrinky-dink thing. Wah-hoh. Check out that smile. This lady could charm the socks off a mongoose.

Martin spoke up. "Miss Jenny, please say 'Hello' to Amelia Starfire, your keeper," he said. Jenny made to say something but nothing came out.

What? Jenny's tongue-tied again?

The giant woman reached down, picked Jenny up in her hand, and lifted her high above the trees. When she spoke, her voice sounded like a water fountain. *At least this keeper doesn't have vocal chords that burst your eardrums.*

"Hello, Jenny!" she said. "I can't tell you how excited I am to be able to talk to you!"

I had to bite my lip. Jen's eyes were like golf balls. *She's doing better than I did. I was scared spitless when Martin first showed up.*

I saw Amelia look down at me then back at Jenny. Then she said, "I am told that you and your brother have been given the gift of seeing the spirit world," she said. "You have no idea what a great privilege this is. I just know the Great One has something magnificent planned. I can hardly wait to see what it is. But you know what the most exciting thing for me is, Jenny dear?"

Jenny shook her head.

"The most wonderful part is that I am now able to talk with you, one on one," said Amelia. "It's a keeper's dream come true."

Jenny still had not said a word.

Amelia's smile got wider and wider, her eyes twinkled, and she began imitating Jenny's trademark habit of wiggling one saucy shoulder then the other.

"Now, don't tell me that you have lost your tongue, sweet thing, because I know better!" she laughed. "There aren't many that can hold their own in a verbal duel with *my* Jenny!"

Then Jenny sprang to life, her shyness melting away like ice cubes on a hot grill. Her words came tumbling out like marbles.

"Are . . . are you really my keeper?" She babbled. "And have you known me all of my life, too? And did you know me even before I was born just like Barry's keeper?"

Ooh-yeah. There's the Jenny I know.

Amelia opened her huge eyes wide and laughed. "Well, the child is not mute after all! Yes, indeed, Jenny. I have been with you from your very first day. One of the privileges of a keeper is getting to watch the Great One put you together from the first teensiest little speck. It's a fascinating process. The Great One is so very particular."

Scrambling to her knees, Jenny shouted, "Amelia, can you shrink yourself down like Martin did? It's kinda windy up here. . . . And your nose is too big for me to hug!"

Amelia actually giggled. "How can I resist such a delightful request!"she said looking down at Martin who was now rolling on the grass laughing again. Who would have guessed that spirits had funny bones?

"Martin," she said, "The tales we'll be able to tell of these two! We'll keep the entire Sky population in stitches for a century!"

She returned Jenny to the lawn and stepped back. Seconds later, Amelia disappeared in a cloud of sparkles. Then a beautiful woman about the same height as our mom stepped out. Like Martin, she still wore her sparkling robes.

We all just looked at each other for several seconds. Then the four of us broke into whoops and giggles. I got a catch in my throat watching my sister shyly reach out for her first hug. Amelia threw her arms around her and rested her pretty chin on top of Jenny's curls.

"Oo-oo, Martin! I could get real used to this!" she said.

Martin placed a hand on my shoulder and said, "I know what you mean, Amelia. This last hour has been one of the most memorable of all my centuries combined. I've found myself laughing just out of sheer joy."

No words can describe how good that felt.

Just then, off in the distance, we all heard a low rumble. As it crescendoed into a roar, a thunderous cracking rocked the ground underneath us.

"Silence! Everyone, be still!" shouted Martin.

CHAPTER 13: SKY BATTLE!

*"Evil will always war against good. The forces of good
will triumph when they recognize and honor
the source of their power."*
~Martin Moonglow

Jenny and I both clammed up, surprised at the fierceness in Martin's voice.

Off in the distance, we heard clicking and swishing sounds. Soon the sky swarmed with thousands of black-winged creatures. At first I thought they were insects because of the flurry and the hissing of their wings. They sounded like a mass of locusts. Wave after wave streamed overhead until they blocked the sun.

Whirling around, Martin spoke to us, his voice firm. "You children stay right where you are," he said. "Do not move a muscle!" He and Amelia, their backs turned to each other, stuck us between them, two slices of salami in a keeper sandwich. Then Martin looked over at Amelia, lifted his head, and shouted, "Stations!"

With a sudden–whoosh!—their bodies exploded into the sky becoming at least as tall as they had been before.

"Look up, Jen," I said. With our eyes nearly popping out of our skulls, we craned our necks upward trying to get a glimpse of the keepers' faces though they were partially hidden by their sparkling silver and blue robes.

"Wow!" said Jenny. "They are so fantastic."

"Yo! Get a load of those four whoppin' feet. They take up most of Grampa's backyard."

I grabbed Jenny's hand and squeezed it. "So," I said, "Did you ever dream you'd see something like this when you crawled out of bed this morning?"

Jenny shook her head. "Never in a million years."

Almost afraid to breath, we tried to stay right where Martin had put us for several minutes. But when both keepers suddenly gave out the most hair-raising roar, our curiosity got the better of us.

At first, we tried sneaking peeks out to the side hanging on to the keepers' robes to keep our feet in place.

"Barry! They have swords! Celestial flame throwers, no less," Jenny shouted.

Just then one of the swords whizzed right past us.

"Jen, look out!" I hollered. Jenny pulled her head back so quickly she landed flat on the ground. I helped her to her feet.

"We're going to be killed, Barry! This is scary!" she cried, sagging against me.

I pulled her face toward me. "Listen! You forget. We have our very own bodyguards. We're not gonna get killed, Jen. Not today."

We stood within the safe confines of the keepers' robes and peered out. Every few seconds one of the flashing swords whizzed by so close we could have reached out and touched it.

"Just where did these giants have their weapons stashed anyhow?" Jen asked.

"Beats me," I said.

We discovered that by pulling the robes back, we could watch the battle overhead and still stay safe.

"They're sure not shy about using those light sabers," I said.

"No duh, Bro."

We watched as the keepers swung the blazing weapons and ripped wide swathes through the hordes overheard. The fire shooting from the swords sent the demons into shrieking retreats. They were forced to scatter in all directions, their formations now in obvious chaos.

"Can you believe this!" I hollered.

Jenny seized my arm. Pointing to the horizon, she shouted, "Look up there!"

From opposite sides of the sky appeared wave after wave of yellow-gold soldier-like beings, riding fiery white-hot chargers. They swooped in and soon had the winged mob surrounded.

"Are they the good guys or more bad ones?"

We got our answer when dreadful screeches erupted throughout the mass of devils. The golden warriors began moving in on all sides and the fiends soon realized they had nowhere to hide. In a mad scramble to escape, they ripped and slashed at each other, screaming and snarling with hair-raising howls. Their yelps alone made our skin crawl.

Jenny clamped her hands over her ears and stomped her feet. "I can't stand to hear those things scream!" she cried. "It's horrible."

But the blazing soldiers pressed their assault, hacking away at any black wing within reach, lopping off a tail here, a limb there. Teeth rattling explosions rocked the sky and thick, black smoke billowed up from beyond the treetops around Grandpa's yard.

"Make it stop! Make it stop!" moaned Jenny. I held her tight. I could tell she was holding by a mere thread.

"We're safe, Jenny, just remember that," I said a little too loudly. *Trying to convince yourself, too, Barry-Boy?*

In a matter of minutes howling forms came hurtling down from the sky, trailing smoke as they fell. Charred bodies smashed to the earth, some landing with sickening thuds right in front of us. Putrid odors rolled off the carcasses. Jenny dug her nails into my arm and began to choke. The smell had me fighting my own gag reflex.

But all this time not once had our keepers moved their feet. Even in the heat of battle, they never shirked their duty to protect us. I realized that, if we had not had spirit sight, we never would have known the danger we were in. For the life of me, I couldn't understand why Jenny and I had to see this stuff.

Jenny was crying by this time. Okay, I'm a guy. I don't do crying girls very well. But I patted her shoulder just the same. She seemed to like that. *I just hope this doesn't give us nightmares. I've already had my share.*

Then, just as quickly as the fray had begun, it was over. The skies cleared, the terrible smells evaporated, and Martin and Amelia returned to normal size.

Jenny and I shivered and our teeth chattered. It was impossible to talk. When Martin and Amelia came over to hug us, we collapsed against them. They held us for several minutes in total silence.

Finally I managed a few syllables. "What *was* that? What just happened?" I choked out.

Martin squeezed my shoulder. "Have a seat, Barry. You, too, Jenny, and we'll try to explain.

"If you'll remember, I told you earlier today that good and bad are always at war. Amelia and I are always on the lookout for danger. Just in the last day or so, we discovered a great evil amassing nearby. We don't know what it is yet, but Amelia and I have been watching it. Something very big. Is that your assessment, too, Amelia?"

She hesitated to answer. "I'm not sure I want to stress these children anymore for today, Martin, but I will ask one question. Was that Measfisto I saw leading that mob?"

Martin nodded. "You saw him too, did you? I haven't seen that beast in over a millennium."

"Trouble is," said Amelia, "You and I both know he never concerns himself with small potatoes. You can be sure that brute is planning something horrific."

"I'm afraid Barry here has already had a run-in with one of his henchmen. Show her your arm, Master Barry," said Martin.

I bit my lip and looked over at Jenny. "Hope you're not squeamish, Jen," I said. "I haven't told you what happened at the video arcade yesterday."

"What do you mean?" asked Jenny.

For the second time that day I pulled up my sleeve and removed the bandages. I heard a sudden gasp. I caught Amelia glancing over at Martin. She mouthed the word "screwtail" and Martin nodded.

"Ee-ew!" said Jenny. "That looks awful. What happened, Barry?"

I launched into a vivid blow-by-blow of my face-off with the monster at the arcade.

"You need to see a doctor, Barry," Jenny said, ". . . like *soon*."

I saw Amelia snap her head sideways at Martin. Then she said, "Children, Martin and I need a private conference. You're not to worry. Even though we are out of sight and sound, we are still right beside you. We are not leaving you alone for a second. Do you understand?"

Jenny and I nodded. But when both our keepers vanished right before our eyes, I still got pretty queezy. I could tell Jenny felt the same.

CHAPTER 14: QUIRKS AND QUIPS

*"In many earth generations, one has to dig under mountains
of family foibles to uncover
the solid core of love hidden beneath."*
~Martin Moonglow

When we heard Mom call us for the second time, I hurried to pull my shirt back down over my arm.

"Does it hurt a lot, Barry?" Jenny asked.

"Yeah. Especially if somebody bumps it," I said. We were both pretty subdued when we stepped inside Grandpa's house.

I saw Mom and Grandma bustling about as they gathered up the party leftovers. Mom worked quietly but Grams can talk the arms off a clock. *She's always like a magpie on steroids*, I thought. Today, she was enjoying her favorite pastime: nitpicking at Grandpa.

"Hanson," she said, "I swear, if you don't quit eating that cake, you won't make it to your next birthday," and, "Did I see you taking a nap right in the middle of the party? You're incorrigible, ya know that? Tsk! How a man can sleep in the middle of the day is beyond me, but with a dozen people talking around him? Unbelievable."

Though Grandpa paid her scant attention, he was the first to notice Jenny and I coming through the door.

"Well, I do have grandkids after all!" he exclaimed. "Where'd you all disappear to? Been missin' ya for hours! Barry, are you done playing in the traffic for today? Come here and give your ancient Gramps a big hug!"

"Happy Birthday, Grandpa!" I said and gave him a big squeeze. Jenny followed suit. *What the . . . ? Is that a keeper's finger resting on Gramps' shoulder?*

I whispered to Jenny. "Hey, did you see that? On Grandpa's shoulder? It's huge!"

She nodded her head. *Hold on to your eyeballs, Jen. They're about to pop loose.*

Mom came up behind me and put her hand on my arm. Just then, Jenny tugged at my sleeve.

"Barry!" she hissed. "What's that?"

I looked up and saw a pink shimmery curtain flowing behind Mom. "Mom must have a keeper too," I said under my breath.

Mom reached up and swiped her hand across my head. "Today, thanks to you, I have a thousand new grey hairs," she said. Then she whispered, "Are you okay?" I nodded.

Grams was another matter. She whirled on me and said, "You sure gave us all a scare, young man! Runnin' out in front of a truck like a chicken with its head cut off. Totally brainless, I'd say." She shook her head and looked over at Gramps. "Gotta admit, though. You come by it honestly. Your grandfather is the king of foolhardy doin's. Tsk! I could write a book."

Then her head snapped up. "Say. I don't believe I saw either you or Jenny with a plate of food. Sylvia, what did you do with all the food? These starving urchins need a sandwich to hold them together for the trip home."

Mom sighed. "Grams, all the food is already out in the car." *Yo. Mom, you look kinda droopy.*

Grandma ignored her. "I'll bet these kids didn't get any cake or ice cream either. Wherever have you been all day? In all my born days, I don't remember any kin of mine being last in line for ice cream!"

Uh-oh. Mom is gonna raise a stink.

"Grams, let's not take the food out again. It'll spoil . . . ." Grandma stopped her mid-sentence.

"Spoil, Schmoil, Sylvia. It's November, for Pete's sake. Besides, if you think you're going to deprive me of the chance to feed my grandchildren at my own table, think again! I don't want to hear another word from you!"

Mom pulled her lips in and whirled away. I caught Jenny's eye and wiggled my eyebrows. Grams handed us our sandwiches. We tucked into them without a word, neither daring to looking at the other for fear Mom would see our eyes dancing. Somehow, Mom had become a little girl again and Grandma had just pinned her ears back. It was too funny.

Jenny leaned over and whispered in my ear, "Isn't it fun to be spoiled by Grams?"

"Yeah," I whispered back, "But even more fun watchin' Mom get so mad she turns purple." Then I proceeded to mimic my mother's pinched lips. Jenny smothered a snort.

But then, something weird happened. As I was putting pepper on my sandwich—okay, I'm a pepper freak—Jenny exploded with a sneeze. But it was her choked out scream that made me look up.

Standing three feet in front of us on the other side of the table was a giant spider, black as pitch. His legs were covered in hair but the hairs were like stiff black toothpicks. His huge, compound eyes, were the size of basketballs. He was standing on his back legs, waving his front legs and clawing . . . at Mom and Grandma!

Then a giant hand reached down from out of nowhere and, with three huge fingers, flicked the huge critter through the wall. It disappeared.

When she could finally speak, Jenny whispered, "What . . . was . . . *that!*" Her voice shook.

"I have no idea."

Neither of us could swallow another bite after that. Even ice cream didn't look good.

"What's the matter with you two?" Grandma demanded.

"Nothin' Grams," I said. "Maybe we're just trying to watch our waistlines like the rest of this family."

Grandma harrumphed.

"Well, not everybody," she said. "I've been workin' fifty years to get that grandfather of yours to *quit* eatin' so much ice cream. He can't go to bed at night unless he's had a great big bowl of the stuff."

Seeing that we were done, Mom shooed us to hurry. Jenny and I were so stunned by the spider we hardly noticed Grandma stuffing cookies into our pockets. *A monster spider the size of a refrigerator . . . in Grandma and Grandpa's house??*

Mom, of course, tired as she was, did not notice that we walked like robots, silent and staring straight ahead. She climbed in behind the wheel and waved. "Mom, Dad. Gotta go. It's been a great day. Happy Birthday, again, Daddy!" she said. "You're just as young as you always were!"

Gramps was quick. "Oh, hog slop! Don't say that too loud or I won't be able to cash in on my Senior Citizen Discount. You'll make me the laughing stock of my buddies. They're taking me to Denny's this Saturday."

Then he leaned over to me and said, "There are definite benefits to bein' 'over the hill', ya know." Then in a stage whisper he said, "Gotta have a few rewards or nobody will opt to live this long! Ha!" Grandpa slapped his knee at his own joke.

When the family had all settled into the car, Gramps started in on his check list.

"When was the last time that you had the oil changed, Sylvia?" and "Are your tires holding up okay?" and "You remember, don't you, never to let the tank get too low on gas?"

I held my breath. Now it was Gramps giving Mom the third degree.

Is the spider going to show up again? I noticed that Jenny kept watching the open door behind Grandma.

Mom listened and nodded. She didn't seem as aggravated as she was with Grams. *She knows she's her daddy's little girl. She also knows that, since Dad died, Gramps has been very protective.* Mom headed him off at the pass like she knew what he was going to ask.

"I'm way ahead of you, Dad," she told him. "Just topped off the tank yesterday." She blew him a kiss and started the car. Then she turned and winked at me with an I-told-you-so swagger.

Jenny sighed.

Gramps whacked the side of the car, his trademark sendoff.

"Get on with ya, now, and don't wait for birthdays to come over and see us. We don't have that many of 'em left, ya know!" We all pretended to chuckle and waved goodbye.

The day was over.

Jenny reached over and almost crushed my hand.

Chapter 15: Conference in the Clouds

"The chain of command in Shomara is composed of love links."
~Martin Moonglow

Meanwhile, the two keepers shot skyward to confer with the Great One. Entering the court, they bowed and called out as they went.

"Oh Great One, we need your advice!"

Then they waited. They knew they were heard, but they also knew that the Great One could postpone answering for eons. Today was different. He answered them immediately.

"Hello, Amelia! And hello, again, Martin! What brings you here?

"Your Majesty, we are here to report great demon activity in the city where our charges live," said Amelia. "Even some prominent tyrants have shown up with their entire entourage."

The Great One listened.

"I know all about it, my dear keepers. I suspect you've come with a request. What is it?"

"Yes, Excellency. As usual, you always know everything," said Martin. "We are wondering whether

Jenny and Barry are in danger, and if we need additional forces to help us protect them. You have given these children spirit sight, so we know that you would not want them in harm's way. We . . . ."

But the Great One interrupted him.

"When did you decide that I wouldn't want them in harm's way, as you put it?"

"But, Your Majesty, they are just children! We . . . we only assumed that . . . ." began Amelia.

"My dear keepers have no fear. You may call on extra protection anytime you want, but I will not allow anything to block the children experiencing what is real. They must know what is real, Amelia, and sometimes that means enduring some pain."

Martin began to sputter.

"But Your Grace, Barry has already suffered some terrible wounds from a screwtail. He's only a boy. Have you ever sanctioned this kind of advanced training for a human this young?"

"No, I have not. You are right, Martin. This is an unusual move, but these are unusual times. The age is coming to a close, and these children must learn the meaning of Truth and learn it with all due haste. I have given them the ability to see the spirit world to speed up that process. In time you will know why I have done this."

The Majesty paused. Then he said, "Your keeper duties remain the same. Protect your charges from death, yes, but you will not be able to protect them from pain."

Martin and Amelia stared at each other, and the Great One chided them.

"Oh, come now," he said. "Do not tell me you cannot understand. It's like parenting."

Again, Martin and Amelia looked at each other with raised eyebrows.

"I realize that neither of you have ever been parents before," the Majesty said. "However, I know you have watched thousands of human families over the centuries. Have you not observed that good parents teach their children how to handle pain? It's a stepping stone to greatness. Having been a parent myself, I have to say it was the hardest job I ever did. Worth every minute, mind you, but still an excruciating experience."

"Yes, Your Majesty. We remember what you went through," said Amelia.

The Majesty's voice took on a cheerful note. "Do not fret my dear keepers! I am watching both you and your little ones. I already know you will do an exceptional job."

"Thank you, O Great One," they answered in unison, and began bowing themselves out of the Great Hall. They had turned to leave when the Great One called them back.

"One more thing, you two. I want you to warn the children that, under no circumstances, are they to give away their secret to anyone, not to any other humans, not to other keepers or spirit messengers, and most important of all, never to the evil ones. Right now, Barry and Jenny are incognito. The spirits do not know that they can be observed by them and I want it kept that way for now."

Again, Martin and Amelia, bowed low. "We understand, O Great Majesty."

As they sped earthward to escort the family car on the busy freeway, Martin was the first to break the silence. "I don't know how you took that, Amelia, but I think we're heading for a major showdown."

"Yes," said Amelia, her voice gloomy. "And The Majesty has the children right in the middle of it."

CHAPTER 16: SLUMBER PARTIES

*"If you understand the Sky World, you know that you are never alone—ever. But whether you realize it or not, you actually **do** choose the company you keep."*
~Martin Moonglow

Home. My feet felt like hundred pound weights. From the time I crawled out of bed this morning to the present, every waking moment had been non-stop confusion. My sister turned me into a super-sized tomato, a strange giant played catch with me a hundred feet above the ground. Then said giant shrank right before my eyes. Then it turned out it was not happening just to me. Jenny was seeing weird stuff too. The "giants" turned out to be keepers whose job it is to protect us. We even saw them in action when we witnessed our first sky battle. And none of that included Martin's mind-boggling rescue when I stepped out in front of that truck this afternoon.

Yeah. I'm tired but I couldn't blame it on the cheesy party or all those senior citizens and their elevator music. My world had been turned upside down. My brain was a bowl of scrambled eggs. As I slogged up the stairs, I met my sister and Amelia. Jenny was chattering like her old self again and I couldn't help eavesdropping.

"I don't have an extra bed for you to sleep in," she was saying. "But I can sleep on the floor and you can have my bed if you like."

I snorted. "She's gonna have to shrink several more inches to fit on that trundle bed of yours, Jenny girl."

Amelia laughed. *Wah-hoh! This lady keeper's gown lights up when she laughs. Cool.*

"Jenny, I'm your keeper! I never sleep. In fact, I'm not even sure how it's done. It's my job to watch over you day *and* night. Your teddy bear and I have occupied the same corner of your room for years. He and I are good friends."

Jenny's eyes flicked open. "Every night? You've been in my room every night of my life?" she asked.

"Yes, Jenny dear!" Amelia said with a smile.

"Oh yippy! Now we can talk all night. How fantastic. Barry, we each have a sleep-over friend every night from now on. This is going to be *so awesome."*

"Hold on there!" Martin whooped. "Let's not get carried away," he said with a laugh. *I really dig his laugh.*

"Yes, not so fast, you two," said Amelia. "Listen, as much as we want to talk with you as well—and there is nothing we would enjoy better—we happen to know that you require sleep. It would never do for you both to get sick on account of us. Now come here, Jenny."

Jenny looked puzzled as she stepped over to her keeper. Amelia placed her hands on either side of Jenny's head, her thumbs on Jenny's eyelids, and left them there for a moment.

"I've done this almost every night of your little life, at just about this time, to help you get to sleep," she said. "Feel tired yet?"

To my surprise, Jenny's head sagged into her keeper's hands. Her head snapped up and she shook herself. "Weird. That's the closest I've ever come to falling asleep on my feet. Barry, you should get Martin to do this for you. My eyelids feel like they're coated with glue." She rubbed her eyes and yawned. "Rats! I had so many questions to ask you."

"Jenny," Amelia said, "We have the rest of your life to talk. You get some sleep, and we'll have a nice chat as soon as you wake up in the morning."

"Guess I'll say g'night then, bro'. You too, Martin," said Jenny, yawning again.

"Goodnight, Jen," I said, stifling my own yawn.

"Have a good sleep, Miss Jenny," said Martin.

Amelia smiled and waved at us, then followed Jenny to her room.

By this time, my arm was throbbing. I slipped into the little half bath close by my room. *Dang! My arm has sure taken some flak today. It's even more swollen than ever.* As I tore the bandages away, washed the wounds and applied salve again, I had to grit my teeth to keep from howling. At last I had fresh bandages but my arm still ached. After brushing my teeth I slogged back to my bedroom.

Martin was there . . . well, sort of. Get this. He sat cross-legged *hovering* six inches above my desk—and the whole upper part of his body was missing. I felt my hair stand up on end. All I could do was stare for five minutes.

When my breathing returned to normal, I sat down on the edge of my bed to wait. I assumed that Martin would have to appear at some point. I had to talk to him even if I had to stay awake all night. Probably wouldn't sleep anyway. My arm was killing me.

But Martin did not reappear. It was maddening. *Spirit sight. Hmph! I don't know any more now than I did before. And now I get to schmooz with a headless body.*

The longer I waited, the grumpier I got. I started pacing back and forth. Every few minutes I kicked my wall. I even threw my pillow across the room.

At last I went over and tapped Martin's arm. His hand went up, palm out, like a stop signal. I jumped back. It was the first movement I'd seen in nearly an hour. Then both hands gave thumbs up signs and Martin made a full-bodied reappearance.

"Hello, Master Barry," he said. Then, all of a sudden . . . "No!"

In a flash, Martin swept something over my head then bounded across the room. I reached up and felt a light filmy cover that I could not clear away. Through it, I could see Martin ripping around my room wiping the walls and ceiling. Every few moments he would act like he was throwing stuff. It was the oddest sight.

At last he stood still in front of me, hands on his hips. He lifted the spidery film off me and said, "I thought you'd be fast asleep by now."

"Where have you been!" I asked, unable to hide how cranky I was. "I'm not tired. I mean, my arm hurts, and I've got a gazillion questions rattling around in my head.

"Master Barry, you are obviously upset. What is your problem?"

I tossed the hair out of my face. "I got mad cuz you were gone so long is all."

"'*Is all*', you say!" shouted Martin, glaring down at me. "Well, for your information, whatever was going on here the last few minutes attracted *demon* activity."

"I don't get it. It didn't see anything."

"I can't explain why you couldn't see it," said Martin. "What I do know is that whatever was going on in your head either leaked out your mouth or had you acting out in anger. Devils cannot read minds but they're masters at watching actions. They've had centuries to figure out when humans are having evil thoughts. Just what were you doing?"

Okay, so it's hard to describe your own juvenile behavior when you think nobody is looking but I did my best. Really. Martin stood and listened, nodding his head. "Well, just so you know, I just cleared your room of a dozen beasties who were salivating over you. Barry, you must learn to control your thoughts."

"Uh . . . right," I mumbled. "So what took you so long? I mean, I was waiting for an hour."

"I was just talking to the Great Prince, Barry," said Martin. "This is all so new to me. I thought it best to check in with him to make sure I'm doing right by you. Imagine my dismay when I come back to find all these devils crawling the walls of your room!"

"Um . . . sorry," I said, clearing my throat. "So does that mean that you're sometimes here and sometimes not here? I mean, I thought you were supposed to protect me."

"Barry," Martin said, "I cannot protect you from making bad choices. I could have stood back and let you take the consequences of your stinkin' thinkin', as you humans put it, but today, I decided to let you off the hook. You've had a rough day."

"Thanks, I guess." Then, I pushed ahead. "Hey, Martin. I was wondering. Can you . . . I mean . . . could you answer a few questions for me?"

Martin smiled. *Whew! I'll take his smile any day to one of his glares.* He put his hand on my shoulder, and settled me back onto my pillow. "Master Barry, like Amelia told Jenny, we have the rest of your life to talk. But right now, your questions will have to wait. You need sleep."

"Blast it all," I muttered. I switched off the lamp by my bed.

What the . . . ? I looked over at Martin. In the dark he lit up like a sunlamp. My room had the brilliance of midday.

"Uh, Martin, is there any way you can turn off that glow-worm thing you do?" I asked. "I mean, we mortals like to sleep in a dark room."

"Glow worm . . . ? Oh-h-h, our sky lighting? Of course, Master Barry," said Martin. "I'll just shrink to a teensy weensy speck of dust and hide under your dresser. Will that work?"

Aching arm and all, that was the last thing I remembered.

CHAPTER 17: THE REUNION

"Nothing brightens the day like the greeting of a close friend."
~Martin Moonglow

Sunday mornings at our house were always chaotic, what with getting ready for Sunday school and attending church afterward. Now this is the scoop: Ever since Dad died, the church families have been there for us. Even before the funeral, people kept showing up at our door with complete meals. Then, over the next few months, folks would come over to mow the lawn or rake leaves. One guy brought his ladder over so he could climb up to clean the gutters. Even now people still drop in, some to bring a hot dish or a pie, some just to check that we're okay.

I have to say that the church folks have been great. Even Jenny agrees. And Mom—Mom raves about them to anybody within earshot. So you shouldn't be surprised when I tell you that Jen and I have this unspoken pact. We don't complain about going to church. When Sunday rolls around, we both get up without a single groan, get dressed, and even make breakfast so Mom has time to get ready herself.

Mom hates to cook on the weekends so she often takes us out to eat when church is over. If you want to know the truth, I think it's her way of thanking us for sitting through boring sermons. And I mean *boring*. Some of them are real snoozers. Jenny and I have a contest to see who can catch the other one falling asleep. Once I lost the bet three Sundays in a row.

But Sunday afternoons is our time. Mom lets Jenny and I do pretty well what we want. We can do homework, (not likely), take a nap (What! Burn daylight lying in bed?), or weed the garden (in your dreams). All she asks is that we keep the house quiet so she can catch up on her sleep.

Sunday afternoons used to be my special time with Dad. Up until today, just the thought of a hike up the mountain or a game of catch brought a lump in my throat.

But today was different. Today we had Martin and Amelia. While Mom rested, Jenny and I slipped away from the house. We wanted to talk out loud to our keepers. It was honkin' great, in fact, pig heaven for two kids starved for adult attention. And our keepers were super. They even took us on a cloud-level tour of the whole city. Riding a hundred feet above the ground was an experience I won't soon forget. We actually walked—well rode—through the clouds. The people below looked like automated toys.

Fall has always been my favorite season. The crisp, frosty air, the smell of leaves, and the colors—wow! They took our breath away. I mean, the trees looked like huge bouquets of orange, red and yellow. I looked over at Jenny and shouted, "Isn't this the coolest way to spend a Sunday afternoon?"

Jenny squealed and yelled, "Yeah! Totally rippin'!"

That's when we heard the music. It was coming from all over the valley.

I saw Amelia look over at Martin.

"Can you hear it, children?" she asked.

"Yes. But where's it coming from? We don't see anything," Jenny called up.

Amelia turned to Martin. "Shall we join them?"

"Absolutely," he said. "You lead the way, Amelia. Touch the air so the children can watch as well as hear."

With that, Amelia swept her great arms out in front of her. In a nanosecond we could see thousands of giant keepers standing all over the city, their arms lifted to the sky, singing. The spectacle blew our minds.

And the music. For some reason it sounded familiar but I had no idea why. All I can say is that it was a combination of a killer rock concert mixed with Metropolitan opera—but even that description didn't fit. But get this: Neither Jenny nor I remember being bothered by the loudness of the music, even though Martin and Amelia were singing at full volume right over our heads. After a while, Jenny and I joined in. I saw Jenny wiping tears several times.

Before we knew it, the sun was setting. The day was over and in a few huge strides, our keepers set us down at our back door.

The moment we walked into house, we heard a voice.

"Hey! Anybody home?"

I looked at Jenny. "That sounds like Chad," I said.

Chad, of course, has been my best friend since early middle school. His family moved here three years ago when Chad's father retired from the military.

As I walked to the front of the house, I wondered how it was that Chad and I hit it off so well. Okay, yeah. We both are nuts about electronics and we have the old making-good-grades thing going on between us. But that's where the similarities ends.

The fact is, we are really different. I'm a ghost—a ghost with red hair, no less. My looks are average at best. Chad, on the other hand, is known at school as "The Face." No kidding. Mugs like his show up in celebrity magazines all the time. And his dark skin—whee-oo! He can lay out on a beach for a week and come back looking like a Greek god. Me? Fifteen minutes even at sunset and I'm a lobster. It is *so not fair*. Add to that, I'm skinny and Chad at thirteen and a half already looks like he belongs in the NFL. No surprise that he's already the school's best football linebacker. The guys on the team call him "Tree Trunk."

But he likes me. I'm the first one he looks up when he gets to school and he's always has his eye out for me if we have different class schedules. I think he likes the way I treat him. I mean, I don't make a big fuss over him like other guys, and I have this teasing thing going on with him almost non-stop. To hear us, you'd think we were arch enemies cuz we're always taking verbal jabs at each other. The truth is, neither of us means a single word. I dunno. I guess it's our secret way of telling the other guy we like him without gettin' all mushy and stuff.

Anyway, I can't tell you how excited I was to see him. I bounded through the hallway door and skidded to a stop. There he stood, dark and tanned like a movie star. Chad was back.

"Hey, you slime ball!" I sputtered, making like I was going to punch him in the arm. "You're supposed to be in Hawaii." Chad feigned surprise.

I stepped back with my arms folded. "Let me guess. You hacked into the hotel's computer system and they threw you out."

"Nope!" said Chad. "Well . . . yeah, but they didn't catch me. That's not to say that they won't find a few surprises on their menu tomorrow, though." Chad wrote his imaginary headlines in the air. "'Eggs Benedict: The surest way to betray your diet.' I just couldn't resist. Too bad I won't be there to see the face of that stuck-up head waiter."

"Okay. Reality check," I said. "What's the *real* reason you're back so soon? C'mon. Spit it out."

Chad sighed and sagged. "Dad got called back on a military emergency," he said. "You'd never guess the man was retired. He says we'll go back to Hawaii another time. But," and here, Chad leaned toward me in a conspiratorial whisper, "If you want my opinion, I think we left because of the new boyfriend Kayla picked up. Dad couldn't stand him."

I snorted and plopped down on a footstool. "Can't your sister go anywhere without reeling in some dopey airhead? She attracts guys like flies to manure."

"Yeah, I know," said Chad, "'cept I liked this one. He had this classy maroon BMW. So sweet. He sure beats out the last one she had. Remember him?"

I nodded. "Yeah," I said, "The one she met on the internet. Didn't she almost run off with him even though she'd never even seen him? And if I remember right, didn't you use some rippin' spy gadget to tap into her e-mail or something?"

"Right," Chad said, sniggering. "That little baby paid for itself in one fell swoop that day. Dad and Mom never did know it was me that tipped them off about Kayla's plan to run away."

"Good thing, too," I said. "That guy was one scary dude. Didn't he talk about blowing up the world? I still can't believe anyone, let alone your sister—a military brat no less—could dream of running off with a virtual terrorist."

"No joke," said Chad. "But hey, this guy over in Hawaii was all right. I wouldn't mind seeing more of him."

Seeing Chad was like a breath of fresh air in a smoky room. The sight of him seemed to take my crazy universe and set it right side up again. Chad and I shared everything. We even had a secret cave hideout up in the mountains that was ours alone. Nobody knew about it except us two guys.

My mom liked him and he loved being at our place. He told me once that he felt like our house was his other digs.

Chad had no problem making himself at home either. I watched him throw himself down on our old couch. "Man, how I love this house," he said.

I snickered. "Whoa, Chaddo! A few more bounces like that and our old sofa will be a pile of splinters."

"Yeah?" he looked up and grinned. "So, what gives around here?" he asked.

At that moment Jenny poked her head around the corner. "Hi Chad," she said. "Gee, you look like you spent several days in a tanning booth."

"Nope," said Chad. "Just a week on a *real* beach."

Jenny rolled her eyes. "Huh. Must be nice. Hey Barry, Mom wants to know if you've got your homework done."

"You can tell her, yes. I did it in study hall at school." When Jenny left, I made a face. "Count your lucky stars you don't have a nosey little sister."

"Big, little—what's the difference? Sisters are a pain in the patootie no matter how old they are," said Chad. Then, changing the subject, he said, "So, did you wear your pajamas to school while I was gone?"

I made a yuck face. "That was two years ago, banana brain, and it wasn't pajamas. It was just a big red sweatshirt."

"Sure looked like pajamas to me," said Chad, snorting. I threw a pillow at him.

Chad laughed. "I just love it when your face turns the same color as your hair."

I rolled my eyes and growled, "I wish you were a computer. I'd delete your entire hard drive in two seconds flat. Then I'd give you a hard reboot. Hey. A reboot would be just the thing right now."

I faked a kung-fu kick at Chad's head. He threw up his arms and howled.

"You wuss," he said with a snigger. "You're just sore 'cause I haven't been around to give you a hard time." Then he heaved a sigh. *Chad getting serious? No way.*

"You gotta know it was no fun in Hawaii without you, Barry. Couldn't tell a soul what I did to the hotel computers. Nobody appreciates my genius like you do."

I pretended to choke and stagger around the room. Then I stopped and said, "Genius, is it? I dunno. There's a fine line between a genius and a lunatic. Let's face it. You're a lunatic."

Chad sent the pillow sailing back and we both laughed so hard our sides ached.

Then it was my turn to get sober. I was dying to tell Chad about my spirit sight. I started to say something, but in one swift move, Martin was in my face.

"No, Master Barry, you are to say nothing to Chad about your spirit sight. Do you understand? Nothing."

I nodded.

All I could say in the end was, "It was no picnic here either. Nobody to hang out with." I looked over at Martin and he gave me a thumbs up sign.

My mind must have drifted because Chad hollered and waved. "Yo! Barry boy. I'm still here. You keep looking over at the corner of the room. Are you seein' ghosts?" Then he chortled at his own joke.

I didn't know what to say. I just stood there. Then I heard the honk of a car outside.

"Uh-oh," Chad said. "My dad's waiting outside for me. Gotta bounce." He slapped his knees and jumped up. "You on for a bike race after school tomorrow?"

"Sure," I said and flexed my arm.

He skip-hopped down the front steps. "See you tomorrow," he called.

Bike ride. Sure. If my arm ever quits hurting.

CHAPTER 18: PAIN AND CONFUSION

"There is always a purpose for pain, but few choose to explore the reasons behind it.
~Martin Moonglow

    I went up to get ready for bed. It was time to check my bandages again. My arm was agony tonight. In spite of all the antibacterial goop, and all the care I had been giving it, the wounds were not getting better. In fact, they were worse. The punctures, now white and puffy, were obviously infected. After completing the bandage ritual once more, I flopped down on the commode lid. Why was this pain not going away? Nothing I did seemed to make any difference.
    That did it. Now I really needed to talk to Martin. The opportunity came the moment I stepped back into my bedroom.
    Martin was again sitting on the dresser, but tonight, he looked like he was waiting for me.
    "There you are, Master Barry. Ready for a good night's sleep?"
    I shook my head. "Not just yet. I have one question to ask you."
    "All right, Barry. One question it is," said Martin.
    I swallowed hard. "Look, Martin," I said, " I've noticed your powers are pretty impressive. I mean, you took care of Jenny's

injury yesterday right on the spot. I was just—well, wondering—could you heal my arm, too? Please? It really hurts. I know this is more than a scratch but it should be no biggie, right?"

Martin looked over at me and said, "Well, Master Barry, I just now finished talking to the Great Prince about that arm of yours. It seems you need to talk to your mother about it."

"My . . . my *mother!*" I exploded. "She knows nothing about my arm – and I don't want her to know, either." *No bleepin' way am I telling Mom about this.*

"Suit yourself, Master Barry! All I know is that your sore arm has something to do with telling your mother something. That's all the Prince would tell me."

I stared at Martin. *Is this bozo for real? If I tell Mom I went to the arcade, I'll be grounded 'til I'm sixty.*

After a moment, I mumbled, "I can't tell my mom." When Martin cocked his head at me, I added, "And no, I don't want to talk about it, okay?"

"Well, Master Barry, whenever you need a listening ear, I'm right here. In the meantime, you better catch some . . . how do you say it? . . . eye-shuts?"

"It's 'shut-eye', Martin," I said. "And with this arm torturing me, I'm sure I won't be sleeping."

"That's too bad, Barry. They say pain will do that to humans," said Martin heaving a big sigh.

So now we're doing the exaggerated "I really care" routine, is that it?

I decided that the least I could do is take a couple of aspirin. After a trip to the bathroom and a couple of swigs of water to down the pills, I tottered back to my bed. Crawling in, I took to pounding my pillow. I looked over at Martin and said, "So you're just going to stay sitting on that desk all night? Don't you have to sleep too?"

He shook his head. "You must not have been listening. Remember when Amelia told Jenny she doesn't sleep? Well, I don't either. The truth is that I've been sitting here every night for several years now. I'll be fine. But thank you for asking."

"Well, don't forget. I need a dark room," I said.

"Oh, right-o," said Martin. "I'll just go find my little hiding place." In an instant, the room went black.

I rolled over and stared at the shadows on the wall, still wide awake. I shifted back over.

"Martin?" I called.

The keeper popped back to normal size and again, he lit up my room. "Yes, Barry?" he said.

"Martin," I began. Then I came right out with it. "Why do I have to tell my mother about being at the arcade? How's that going to cure my sore arm?"

Martin leaned back against the desk and folded his arms. "Maybe I should ask you a question," he said. "Did your mother know you went to the arcade? She always knows where you are, right?"

I paused then mumbled, "No, she didn't know where I went that day."

Martin's eyebrows went up. "Oh-h-h . . . . So, am I to understand that you did not have permission to be at the arcade?"

"Yeah, I guess."

Okay. This conversation is going from bad to very bad.

"But you knew this all along, right? You're just asking these questions to make me feel bad. I mean, you've been with me since birth so you know everything about me. Isn't that so?"

Martin lifted his chin and stared me straight in the eye. "Have you forgotten what I told you about your episode at the arcade? I was not there. Somehow the demon world cloaked you from my sight. Again, I repeat. I was not there. I do not know what happened."

"Oh."

Martin nodded his head. "And as I see it, Barry, your arm is going to stay sore until you confess to your mother about it. That wound is there to remind you that you have something you need to do. Your mother may not know of your actions but the Great Prince does. He sees everything. He knows that you need to make things right with your mother."

Martin cleared his throat then went on. "Master Barry, I am not just whistling in the wind here. Even though I begged the Prince several times, he refused to heal your arm. He said, 'No. Not until the boy speaks with his mother.'"

I threw myself back onto the bed, my hands over my face and Martin's words ricocheting in my ears. I felt like a boat anchor had landed on my chest. *Why does this always happen to me? Mom warned me about the arcade. I just hate it when she's right.*

I rolled over and looked at the keeper. "Okay," I muttered, "I'll tell her first thing in the morning."

At that moment there was a knock on the door.

"Barry?" It was Mom calling outside my door. "Barry, you have a phone call."

I got up and opened the door.

"A phone call?"

"Yes, dear," Mom said. "I know it's late, but it's Chad and he seems pretty upset." She handed me the phone.

I grabbed the phone and said, "Chad? You okay?"

Chad didn't answer for a moment. When he spoke, his voice sounded gravelly.

"Barry, I'm so scared." He was whispering so low I could barely hear him. "I don't know who to talk to. I just found out somethin' really bad."

"Speak up, Chad. Do you want me to come over?" In the background, I could hear him snuffling. *Chad crying? Must be somethin' pretty awful.*

"Chad, I can't hear you. Can you come over here?" I asked. "We could talk in my dad's woodshop. It's warm and private."

"Yeah, I guess. I'll be there in ten."

In nine minutes and thirty seven seconds, Chad was standing on my doorstep. Without a word, he made a bee line for our woodshop, went in and shut the door behind us.

"So, what's going on?" I asked. "What's happened? You were fine a half an hour ago."

Chad began by saying, "Well, Dad and I were on our way home, see? And Dad recognized somebody walking on the sidewalk across the street. He said he needed to go talk to this guy, right? So he parked real quick and got out of the car."

"Yeah?"

"Yeah," said Chad. "And, well, I guess when he got out of the car, he must've dropped his cell phone 'cause it started ringin'."

"So?"

"Well, at first, I just let it ring. But when it kept ringing I went looking for it. It was between the driver's seat and the door."

"And?"

"Well, I was going to take it out to Dad, but I couldn't see him in the dark, so I decided I would answer it just like Dad always does. You know. All he says is, 'Yeah.' So that's what I did. Just swiped it open and said, 'Yeah.'"

"Uh-huh. Then?"

"Well, I guess the guy on the other end must've thought I was

Dad, 'cause he says . . ." Chad's voice started to crack. ". . . Barry, he says, 'Sorenson, we think the Mother Load is being moved. We need to grab it before anybody figures out that we know about it.' Then he hung up, just like that."

I didn't know what to say. Chad dug the heels of his hands into his eye sockets. We were both quiet for a long time. Then, in an effort to get the conversation going again I said, "Listen, Chad. Didn't you tell me once that your Dad had special military duties?"

"Yeah," Chad whispered.

"Well, maybe this is one of those assignments," I said.

"I don't think so, Barry." Chad sniffled again. "My dad never messed with money and stuff."

"But what else could it be, Chad?"

Then Chad couldn't hold back his sobs.

"Barry! I'm scared my dad's gone bad! I've heard of retired military guys that go rogue. You know. After they leave the military, they use their skills to do illegal stuff."

I whirled around and stood in front of him. "Chad, you've been watching too many movies. Your dad would *never* do that!"

Again, Chad was quiet. He wiped his nose on his sleeve. "I wish I knew, Barry. Sometimes I think I don't even know my dad."

I felt for my buddy. How many times I'd heard him say that he wished he had a dad like mine, one that stayed home for more than a month at a time. Now I didn't even have a dad. All of a sudden, I couldn't breathe.

I coughed. "Look, Chad," I said. "This has to be one of your father's special operations. You know your dad loves his country and his family. He would never betray it—or you. You know that. Ya gotta trust him."

"I dunno, Barry. I wish I could be sure." Chad got up abruptly and left. As he walked away into the night, I could hear him sobbing way down the block.

Chapter 19: The Confession

*"Failure to accept responsibility for one's actions is like spitting into the wind.
You always end up with slobber on your face."*
~Martin Moonglow

When I woke up the next morning I had this nagging sense that something was wrong. Yeah, I know. Duh.

"Hello there, Master Barry!" Martin said with a grin. *Great. Just what I need. Mr. "Joy in the Morning."*

I mumbled, "Mornin'" trying at the same time to focus my eyes on his face. *Okay, I know there's something I have to do. Drat. Why can't remember? My head feels like a jumble of knots. Come on brain, pull it together.* Rolling over, I made to get out of bed, and winced.

"Aw!" I moaned. "My arm."

Then it hit me. Like a locomotive barreling through my body, I remembered. *Today's the day I have to tell Mom about the arcade.* The accumulated misery of the last few days crushed me like an empty soda can. I groaned. Doomsday had arrived. *Why do I suddenly feel like a rat has gnawed a hole in my stomach?*

"Martin, have you seen my mom yet?" I mumbled.

"No, Barry, not yet," answered Martin. "Are you okay today?"

"No, I'm not okay," I answered through clenched teeth. "My arm is killing me, and my stomach is in knots."

"So, what are you going to do about it, Master Barry?" Martin asked. *Okay. Like, on the "Idiotic Question" scale of one to ten, that's gotta be a seventeen....*

I ran my hands through my hair then pulled myself upright.

"Guess I'm gonna have to face the music," I whispered as I shuffled off to the bathroom. Under my breath I growled, "Where's a Pied Piper when I need one?"

I splashed some cold water on my face, and checked the dressings on my arm. I was already beginning to bleed through the bandages so I took the time to change them again.

The sooner I get this over with, the better.

When I returned to my room, Martin confronted me.

"Master Barry," he said, "One thing you need to know before you talk to your mother. You are not to tell her—or anyone—about your spirit sight. The Majesty was very particular about that when I last talked to him."

"This Majesty guy is sure pi...," I started to say.

Martin cut me off. "Barry, I beg of you!" he said. "It's not wise to cross the Majesty."

"Okay," I said. I was already feeling like pond scum. "Relax. When I tell my mom that I went to the arcade she's going to take a blow torch to my hide as it is. If I told her I was seeing weird creatures like you and Amelia, she'd haul me off to a shrink quicker 'n snot."

I gave Martin a pat on the shoulder. "You and the Majesty have nothing to worry about," I said. Under my breath, I muttered, "I just wish *I* had nothing to worry about."

I dressed with great care. *So this is what death row inmates feel on the day of execution.* Dragging myself down the stairs, I slid into a chair at the kitchen table. Mom sat across from me nursing her morning coffee.

"Good mornin', big boy! Are you all ready for this day?" she asked.

I started to talk but choked. *Did I just swallow a pin cushion?*

Mom waited for a moment, then asked, "You feelin' okay?"

I blinked and said, "No. Uh-h... I mean, my pillow seemed lumpy last night. I didn't sleep a wink." *Oh, way ta go, Barry.*

Another lie. Your pillow has nothing to do with you not sleeping, and you know it.

Mom chuckled. "Well, if I remember right, Columbus brought that feather pillow over with him on the Mayflower. Would you like me to get you a new one today? We'll give that ratty one a toss."

"Uh-h, yeah. Thanks, Mom," I said. *Why does she have to be so confounded nice all of a sudden?*

Mom cocked her head to the side. "So, do you feel like cinnamon rolls this morning, or do you want some scrambled eggs?"

"I'm not hungry right now," I said. *At least that's the truth.*

I saw Mom's eyes fly open. *Oo-oo-boy. She's onto me already.* Before I could react, she reached over and put her hand on my cheek. "Now I know you're not feeling well," she said. "You never turn down breakfast."

I felt like I had a choke chain around my neck. *C'mon. She's waiting. Spit it out before you barf.*

"Mom, I'm okay, but . . . but I have to tell you something." I saw Mom sit back and look at me, her face serious.

"What's that, Barry," she said.

I took a deep breath. *Okay. Now or never.* "Well, you know how you always told me you didn't want me going to the video arcade?"

"Ye-e-s . . . I've said that several times," said Mom.

"Um, well . . . uh . . . ." *C'mon Barry. Out with it.* "Okay, I've been going anyway, behind your back. You didn't know." I took a deep breath. Then I added, "I'm sorry, Mom. You were right. It's not a safe place."

Mom was quiet for a full minute. I wondered what she was thinking. *Probably planning several decades worth of slave labor between now and when I'm carted off to a nursing home.*

"Hm-m," said Mom. "To tell you the truth, son, I've already known about this. Are you aware that Darla down the street works at the Chocolate Factory in the mall? She told me that she saw you down there a day or two ago. Came as quite a surprise to me, Barry. I have been wondering how long it would be before you told me the truth."

All I could do was just stare at her. *She already knows! Now I'm boiled zucchini for sure.*

"Barry, how did you feel when you disobeyed me like that?" Mom asked.

Lemme think. Um-m . . . peachy?

I heaved a huge sigh. "Rotten."

Mom nodded. "I knew there was something wrong because you've been so grumpy lately. After what Darla told me, I suspected that your conscience was getting to you."

She was quiet for another full minute. Then she said, "Barry, you know that disobedience has consequences, don't you?"

I felt my chin drag on my chest. *Now I'm in for it. She's gonna grind me up for mincemeat.*

Mom took her time. Then she said, "Barry, I have decided to sell your bike."

I snapped my head up.

"What!" I exclaimed. "Mom. Mom please! Make it some other punishment but not my bike. You . . . *you can't sell my bike!*"

"Well, son, now hear me out," Mom said. "If it hadn't been for the freedom that you had because of that bicycle, you would not have been able to go to the mall. As I see it, you had a privilege and you abused it. You used your bike to go places against my wishes."

I felt like I had been hit by a nuclear bomb.

But Mom wasn't through.

"From now on, Barry, you will be taking the bus to and from school. Beginning today, you will report to me the minute you come in the door after school. Do you understand?"

Okay, I knew a confession would be hard, but I never expected this. I kept my eyes trained on the floor.

CHAPTER 20: THE GATE

"At the right time and the right place, a new experience can open up a whole new world."
~Martin Moonglow

I was dumbfounded. How could she take away my bike! Not now, just when Chad was back. That bike was my pride and joy. I felt my whole life crashing down around me. What'll I tell everybody? I'll be a nobody again. All my hard work over the years to fit in with the guys had just been dumped into the trash bin. No more group rides with the crowd. No more races with Chad in the park . . . . And all because of a few visits to a video arcade. It wasn't fair!

"You haven't answered me yet, Barry," said Mom.

I turned away so my mom wouldn't see my rage. Then I growled, "Yeah, I get it." Without another word, I got up and tromped upstairs to my room. Martin was there waiting for me, but I was in no mood to talk. Grabbing my books, I stuffed them into my backpack, slung my jacket over my shoulder, and ran back down the stairs. I punched open the front door and slammed it hard behind me.

Martin did not follow me.

When I got to the bus stop, I stomped my feet to keep the circulation going. Dang. It was way too early for the school bus. And, of course, it had to be colder than an Eskimo's icebox out there. I pummeled my arms with my fists. Dag nabbit it! I couldn't go back to the house now. But waiting for a bleepin' bus . . . this was *so* not-fun. I was turning into a block of ice. Gotta keep moving.

I kicked a rock. It bounced onto the road and landed on the far side of the street.

Wait a minute. If I took shortcuts, I could make it to school in fifteen minutes. I launched out across an open lot with a bitter November wind scouring my head. I yanked my jacket collar up around my ears. *Blasted wind chill. I'll be a hoar frost bunny before I get half way there.* The more I thought about losing my bike, the more I seethed. The injustice of it all!

Then an idea struck me. I stopped right in the middle of the field. Why should I go to school? What was the point? It was always the same boring brain mush every day.

I slammed my fist into my hand. "I'm skippin' school!" I shouted out loud.

Then, through chattering teeth, I muttered, "Right, Barry Boy, and just where do you think you're gonna go?" I knew I couldn't just show up at any of my friends' houses. They would all be in school. If I went back home my mom would tear into me big time. Mom didn't have to be to work for another hour and the bank where she worked was not that far from the house. She could zip home on her breaks for any number of reasons. Nope. Going home was out of the question.

Gramps! I'll go over to Grandma and Grandpa's house. Somehow, I'll find a way to stay out of sight over there. Yeah. I am so out of here.

Ramming my hands deep into the pockets of my jacket, I turned on my heels and set out at a brisk pace. Even though my grandparents lived just ten blocks away, I knew they were long blocks. It was a still a good twenty minute walk.

My mind was racing now. I had never skipped school in my whole life. By the time I got to my grandparents' house I was having second thoughts. *Okay. I can't knock on the door. Grandma will wonder why I'm not in school. If she calls Mom, I'll get my hide nailed to the kitchen door. Nope. I'll hunker down in Grandpa's special room.*

I knew about Gramps' secret hideaway out in his tool shed. He often snuck back there when he couldn't take Gram's nagging anymore. He had it fixed up pretty nice, too, his own TV, his radio, a stuffed recliner, and a bookshelf full of his favorite shoot-'em-up-and-dead-'ems. I just hoped the heater was working.

I slipped around the north side of my grandparents' house, the side that had only two small windows, and took the long way around to enter the shed. But when I tried the door, it was locked.

"Drat it all!" I growled, yanking at the handle. The whole world was against me today. As I stood there, I started to shiver again.

"Sheesh! If I don't exercise I'll freeze solid," I muttered.

First, going behind the shed, I set my backpack down away from my grandmother's eagle eye. My grandmother can walk by a window and catch even the smallest detail out of place. My backpack would give me away in a heartbeat.

To stay warm, I jogged in place for several minutes and slapped my hands together. When my hands turned red and puffy I had to stop. But now, at least, I had some circulation going. I found an old stick lying under the hedge that grew around the perimeter of Gramps' yard. I picked it up and, stepping behind the bushes, I walked along the fence letting my stick clack the boards as I went. It was an old trick I had learned years ago. It seemed to settle my nerves. Rickety-rack, rickety-rack, rickety-rack. *Think, Barry, think.* Rickety-rack, rickety-rack, rickety-rack, rickety-rack . . . *thud.*

Thud? I stopped and stared. What was that? I scanned the fencing, but I couldn't see much of it. Grandpa's old fence was shrouded in thick ivy.

Now, I admit it. I love mysteries and there was something peculiar about that fence. I began pulling away some of the old vines.

"Criminy. This stuff is tough," I muttered, breathing hard. "Gramps, you need a weed whacker back here."

Finally, I could see what had caused the thudding sound. It looked like an old gate. I pulled at my lip. *I've been scraping along this fence for years. How come I've never found this gate before?*

I wanted to open it but a there were still a lot of dead brush in the way. I blew on my hands to warm them up. "Here goes," I said and tore into the shrubbery with a vengeance, whipping up my anger over Mom's heavy-handed verdict that morning. The fence was so overgrown that I worked a good quarter of an hour before I could see the entire gate.

"Whew! What a mess," I said, puffing hard. Then I stood back to get a good look at it.

The gate was beautiful in a weird sort of way. I mean, it was a work of art. But it looked so out of place in Grandpa's ordinary fence. The more I brushed the weeds and dust away, the more I could see that the piece was expertly carved. I ran my fingers over the lines—trees, lakes, deer, wolves, and bears—all created with great precision. Wow. I doubt even my woodshop teacher could turn out something this amazing, I thought to myself. Toward the top, hovering above the scene I could make out a strange bird, sculpted to look like an eagle but with a magnificent, feathered crown and a long, flowing tail.

I scratched my nose. Why had such a fancy piece been built into this plain old fence? And why let weeds cover something that belonged in an art museum? It made no sense.

I wondered what was on the other side.

I scanned the gate for a way to open it. I found a rusty latch but when I lifted it, nothing budged.

"Yuckers," I muttered. "I need some kind of tool, something hard to wedge into that crack." Walking a little ways along the fence, I spotted an old metal brace located high up on the support boards. I picked it up and turned it over in my hands. It was a bit warped, but it would work. Back at the gate I used a rock to ram the brace into the small crack between the gate and the fence. Then, with all my strength, I pushed sideways on the metal brace. The gate began to move, creaking and groaning on rusted hinges.

In a few minutes, I had opened up a gap just wide enough for a leg and an arm. Worming my chest into the opening, I finally managed to squeeze the rest of my body through. The moment I cleared the gate, it shut behind me with a loud clang.

At first, all I could see was dense shrubbery. But I followed the light filtering through the leafy canopy above until I stepped out into blazing sunlight.

I could not believe what I saw.

"Whoa! Some backyard!" I whispered.

I was standing on the edge of a hill. The valley that stretched out before me was, well, like a picture right off a calendar.

This can't be real. I rubbed my eyes. In all my life I had never seen such lush landscaping. Rolling hills of jade-colored velvet stretched out for miles, giving way to dark, rich forests that nestled at the base of purple-hued mountains. There was even snow on the mountain tops. And was that a river wandering across the plain? I couldn't make it out except that hundreds of flowering bushes seemed to be blooming along its banks, a garland of flowers flung across a bed of green silk. (Okay, who says poetry is dead?) But I figured there was a river when the flowering trees ended at a cliff and a stunning waterfall tumbled into a deep emerald pool below.

Wait a minute. Where are all the houses? What happened to the neighbors? Where's the rest of the city?

I looked down at the pool. Maybe there was something down behind those trees by the water.

I looked back toward my grandfather's fence but thick shrubbery hid it. For some reason, I felt a prickly sensation along the back of my neck. Why can't I see any of the town? If I wander too far will I be able to find my way back? I shrugged. Surely I could use this waterfall and the pool here as landmarks.

As I surveyed the hill, I saw a small path that twisted along the grassy slope. It ended at the water's edge below. Tucked under the branches of the trees overhanging the water I could even make out a secluded little beach.

I noted another weird detail. The air seemed milder on this side of the gate. I mean, for a November day it felt more like early summer—not too hot, not too cold. I rubbed my head. *My jacket is going to get way too warm.*

As I picked my way down the slope, the ground between the rocks was so mossy that it felt like sponge. Stepping on it was like walking on new carpet. A light breeze perfumed by hundreds of blossoms wafted up to me.

All of a sudden, I laughed at the top of my lungs.

"Oo-oo yeah!" I hollered. "What a great day to skip school!" No more marching from class to class like a mindless lemming. No teachers breathing down my neck. No silly multiple choice tests that twisted my brain into a pretzel.

As I took a deep breath, my eyes again lit on the pool below. It was so clear I could almost see the bottom of it. Wow! Chad and I could have so much fun swimming in a place like this. Such great diving spots.

About halfway down the hill, I heard a loud screech in the sky and turned to see what it was. A huge bird flew toward me. It had a long tail like the bird carved on the gate and I was mesmerized just watching it come closer and closer.

Then, from out of nowhere, a sudden flash of light hit me full in the face. Disoriented, I lost my balance and stumbled backward. With no time to think, I twisted around and stretched my arms out to break my fall—but my hands never touched the grass.

Instead, with a head-spinning swoosh, my jacket tightened around my chest and I felt myself yanked into thin air. Something screamed overhead and I heard the sound of flapping wings.

Then I knew. I was in the clutches of the long-tailed bird! I had been snatched up like a field mouse. I tried to struggle, but my efforts were useless. The powerful bird had a solid grip on me. I could feel the sharp tips of its talons scraping my bare back every time I twitched. Its claws must have slashed right through my leather jacket in one slice. Whenever I tried to jerk around, they dug right into my skin. I had to force myself to go limp.

Then I made another terrifying discovery. *I couldn't see. I was totally blind!*

The last thing I remembered was that flash of light. Now I could see nothing, no light, no shadows. The realization set me screaming at the top of my lungs.

"Somebody help me, please! Somebody help!"

CHAPTER 21: THE NEST

"If humans could smell the air when they dabble in wickedness, they would flee the stench."
~Martin Moonglow

I felt my body go hot and cold. What was happening to me? How could I have been struck blind? What kind of creature was this that snatched me? Where was it taking me? Was I going to die?

Since I could no longer see, all my other senses went on full alert. All of a sudden I was aware that my fingers were losing their feeling in the cold air. My body felt like a giant goose pimple. *We must be climbing into the upper atmosphere because the temperature is dropping.* The bird's claws against my back were feeling more and more like shards of ice. Then the wind picked up and freezing needles of arctic air seeped into every tiny crevice of my jacket.

Gasp! I can't breathe!

Not only was the air getting colder, but it was getting thinner. My ears strained for any new sound but all I could hear was the flapping of huge wings above me. The frigid temperatures set my teeth to chattering. Then I remembered I had a keeper.

"Mar . . .!" I tried calling to him, but my voice stuck in my throat.

Some keeper you turned out to be, Martin baby. Isn't it your job to protect me from stuff like this? Where are you when I need you? What a cruddy time to do a disappearing act.

Then I began to worry. Just where was this giant pterodactyl taking me? Does it have a nest or will it just drop me into some rocky chasm and leave me to die?

Okay. The nest thing bothered me. Would there be super-sized chicks in it? Maybe they're waiting to tear pieces of flesh off my body. *I'll be eaten alive. I'm going to be bird lunch!*

As the air grew even colder and thinner, I began to drift in and out of consciousness. I fought to stay awake but I must have gone completely under because I woke with a start. The bird had let go of me.

I'm falling! "No-o-o!"

Then what seemed like an hour later, I landed—kwump!—on something that squeaked like my grandfather's rattan rocking chair. I grunted on impact, my mouth wide open. That was a mistake because I ended up with a whole face full of . . . of fluff.

"Yech!" I began to spit and spit some more. Feathers? Yeah. I guess birds really do line their nests with feathers plucked off their own bodies. I had "spitting" proof.

"Br-r-r!" I stuttered through clicking teeth. "Even Gramps' back yard wasn't this cold." Pungent odors surrounded me. They reminded me of the chicken coop our neighbors had years ago, a mixture of bird droppings, feathers, and dried grass. I shoved my nose into my jacket. The smell of my mom's laundry detergent brought a lump to my throat. Would I ever see my family again? Tears spilled down my cheeks. I had never felt so alone.

But wait. What about the chicks? I knew they could be within easy pecking distance. I lay stock-still listening. Even the slightest movement made the nest creak and groan like it was alive. I laid still not even wiggling a toe. The only thing I heard was silence.

Okay. One more test. With a quick sweep of my arms and legs I spread my body out in every direction. Then I went dead still again and held my breath. Nothing.

Whew! I was the only one in the nest. This could be good and it could be bad. Good in that I will not be the next meal for a bunch of oversized baby birds. Bad because I was still alone, hungry – and blind.

Just how do blind people figure out their surroundings? I needed to know where I was. At first, all I heard were leaves rustling in shrubbery nearby. After a minute I heard a screech reverberate off rocky walls in the distance. Uh-oh. The bird was still out there.

That's bad. But then I heard the eerie howl of a wolf. Hm. That's really bad. I shivered and curled my knees up to my chest.

There was no getting around the obvious. Wherever this place was, it was freezing cold, it was full of scary noises, and the sticks under me were not designed for human comfort. My blindness also ensured that I would stay stuck in this place.

I had never imagined what it would be like not having use of my eyes. In fact, I was not sure I had ever even met a blind person. Now I was one. All I had to depend on was my sense of smell, touch, and my hearing. I stretched out my arms to explore my surroundings. Everywhere I turned all I could feel was feathers.

"Feathers. Nothing but feathers," I muttered. I spit out a quill. You'd have thought that a hundred pillows had burst. But things could have been worse. I could be fighting the giant bird, but so far, Big Bird hadn't come back for me. I hoped it would stay gone. I needed time to think.

But without warning, all the events of the last week welled up inside me and I yelled at the top of my lungs.

"Aw-w-w!!"

Even if I got out of this alive, I'd never be able to do anything again. I buried my head in a pile of feathers and let the tears take over. I'd never be able to walk by myself again. I'd never ride my bike, or go swimming again. And my so-called spirit sight? What a crock. My keeper had evaporated. I was a dud anyway. Useless for the "Majesty's" big plans, if indeed there were any plans.

I sat up and began talking to myself out loud. The sound of my own voice was somehow a comfort, maybe because it was the last link to the only world I knew.

"So where am I?" I muttered. "I'm in a bird's nest. But what's on the outside of it? If I crawl out of this nest, will I fall over a cliff?" The nest had to be high up on a mountain. The air was so cold.

I began scrambling about the nest on all fours to feel how big it was. By the time I had crawled my way all around it, my face and hands were scraped raw by sharp twigs woven into the nest.

Ei-eech! Blind people must be covered with scratches and bruises all the time.

Then I heard the flap of wings. Something settled in front of me and the nest rocked like a ship on high seas. I could feel the warmth of a live body close by and I noticed that it was big enough to block the cold wind.

So, the bird is back. Death on two wings. What will it feel like to be picked apart by a bird of prey? Guess I'll find out in a few seconds. No use fighting it.

I sucked in a lung full of air and held it. Then I hunkered down and braced myself for the end. Nothing happened. Nothing, that is, until I felt the bird's wing hit the top of my head. Ow! This was it. That sharp beak was gonna rip into me anytime now. But no. The giant bird seemed to be settling into the nest. As it folded its wings I was caught beneath one of them. Rather than crawl away from it, I tucked myself into a tight ball and rolled toward the heat of its body. I didn't even care if it was only for the final few minutes of my life. At least I'd be warm.

When the great wing finished folding, I found myself trapped under it. At first the bird seemed restless and shifted its weight several times but soon it stopped. I waited, not daring to stir. Then the bird went quiet.

Yo. I don't get it. Isn't Godzilla the Peacock hungry? Why is it going to sleep? Must be that it ate before it came back to the nest.

I nearly choked on the air under that wing. *Phew! You need a bath, Big Bird.*

All of a sudden a chilly blast of wind found me and I flinched. *Br-r-r! I need more feathers.* Taking great care not to wake the bird, I reached out and scooped in several armfuls of soft down to cover my feet and legs. Then, bit by bit, I worked myself around until I was right next to the bird's body. My feet and hands soon began to get some circulation in them.

That didn't mean that my sore arm stopped hurting. In fact, the pain was brutal at times. Mentally, I shut it down hard and forced myself to concentrate on something else. My stomach reminded me that I had stomped out of the house that morning with very little breakfast. *What I wouldn't give for a ham sandwich right now.* I could have kicked myself for being so bullheaded. Now, I was cold, blind, nursing an infected arm, and hungry to boot. I knew I would never sleep. That was my last thought before I lost consciousness.

I woke to discover I was enveloped in feathers from head to toe. The bird was gone. I was surprised at how warm my feather bed was. I was even more surprised that I was still alive. *Is it day or night? How do blind people judge the passing of time? And how long have I been sleeping?*

Add to that, I was now really hungry. Was this the beginning of starvation? I wondered what my mother was fixing for breakfast right now. Hold on. Maybe it was evening time now. That would mean that Mom was cooking dinner. Maybe she was baking her famous pork chops at this very moment! My mouth watered. How I would love to be sitting down for a family dinner with a pork chop and applesauce on my plate looking across the table at my mom and sister.

Funny how what seemed so trivial to me before now took on great importance. I pictured Jenny diving into her mashed potatoes and talking a blue streak to whomever would listen. In spite of myself, I snorted. Did she know that her pigtails flopped around when she talked? I missed the little family routines I would never see again—my mother putting laundry into the washer, my sister talking on the phone with a friend, my mom pouring herself another cup of coffee while she stood at the stove. Tears sprang unbidden to my eyes. Everyone I loved had been ripped away from me! First Dad, now Mom and Jenny.

I sat up with a jerk. Did anyone know I was gone? Did Mom and Jenny know I was missing? And again, where *was* Martin? Why couldn't a giant as powerful as Martin take out a simple bird? I shook my head. *Not part of your job description, is that it, Martin?*

The realization hit me like a steel cabinet dropped from ten floors up. I had been deserted. I was on my own. A frosty finger of fear raced up my spine and my breathing turned ragged. I was doomed! I would never sleep in my own bed again or hug my mom. I would never tease my sister or talk with Chad even one more time. Once again, my stomach rumbled and I groaned. Never would I enjoy Mom's roast beef dinner again.

"Face it, Barry," I sobbed out loud. "In your condition, what good are you really? Even if you do survive, you're going to be blind from now on. You'll have to depend on everyone around you for the simplest needs. No more lizard hunts with Chad on the mountain. No more quiet walks with Mom and Jenny picking up chestnuts in the fall. I'll never see another sunset over the Ozarks.

What had my life amounted to, anyway? So I was the only kid in school with an "A" average for six years in a row. Big deal! My whole life had been a waste. I dug my fists into my eyes. "Here

I am, stuck in a bird's nest up thousands of feet on a mountain. Even the FBI won't think to look for me up here."

I howled into the blackness. "Barry Klutzinheimer here, about to become the main course for some huge eagle!" I burst into tears and slumped to the floor of the nest. "This is it. This is the end."

Soon, I was so hungry I was cramping. I couldn't decide which hurt worse, my arm or my stomach. I had no clue how long I had been in the bird's nest. I only knew that my stomach felt like it was scraping my back bone.

"Awrgh-h-h!" My voice bounced off canyon walls below.

When my stomach growled again I was sure I heard that echo too.

CHAPTER 22: RELIEF FROM AN ODD CORNER

> "In a situation that seems hopeless, help can arrive
> from a unexpected source."
> ~Martin Moonglow

Then, out of my blackness, the sound of beating wings, faint at first, grew louder and louder. I swallowed hard. *The bird is back.* I just sat there. Whatever this monster had planned for me, it was obvious that I had little choice in the matter. The nest lurched as the great beast landed on the edge. The twigs of the nest creaked under the extra weight.

All of a sudden, a warm object landed in my lap. Criminy. Now what? I froze. If it was something alive, a mouse or a live rabbit, it would soon scurry off. But nothing moved.

Then a wonderful aroma hit my nose. Bread! I put my hand down and felt a warm, round loaf. Oh, wow! It smelled better than Christmas dinner. I tore off a huge chunk and gulped it down.

A thought niggled the outer edges of my brain. *What if this is my last supper?* I shrugged. If it was, so be it. The bread was still delicious. In fact, it was the best meal I had ever tasted.

The nest wobbled and squeaked again and I heard the great wings catching the wind again. The bird was back in no time bringing something else that it tossed at my feet. This time it was a sponge filled with water. I sucked on the sponge and drained it dry.

I hadn't realized I was so parched. With my stomach full, and my thirst quenched, I settled back down in the feathers and slept again.

This began a strange pattern. The giant bird brought me bread, water, and even a piece of *cooked* meat every now and then. *Okay, that's weird.* I spent the rest of my time either sleeping, trying to keep from freezing, or pondering my fate. Once in a while, the bird would spend some time in the nest, tucking me in close under its wing to keep me warm. Never did it attempt to harm me. *Double weird.*

So here's the truth. At first, I was so focused on food, water, and staying warm that I didn't even question the bird's abnormal behavior. I know that's hard to believe, but there it is.

But hoo-boy! The moment I gave myself permission to think about *why* the bird was acting so strange, questions crowded into my head like a swarm of yellow jackets at a cookout.

Okay, since when does a bird of prey care two pin feathers about its victims? How does it know that I'm hungry, thirsty, or cold? For cryin' out loud, we're talking predator here, aren't we? Don't predators eat anything they get their claws into? I moaned and shook my head. Nothing made sense. In fact, I realized I was several ideas short of a clue.

A new thought hit me. Maybe I was just part of some creepy experiment. Wait. Was I a guinea pig? Was somebody trying to figure out what a bird of prey is capable of doing? But why use me, a live kid, to test a bird's ability to follow orders? That's pretty sick. At that point, I felt like I was going crazy.

I came to only one conclusion. "I can't go on like this anymore," I muttered. "I have to escape. I have to try to get off this mountain."

CHAPTER 23: ESCAPE PLANS

"All living creatures must come to terms with the fact that they are not in control of their own destinies."
~Martin Moonglow

The prospect of being the bird's next meal never left my mind. "I have to get away. Anything is better than being ripped to shreds by this monster. If there is a lunatic bird-trainer in the mix I am *so* outa here."

The more I thought about it, the more I managed to convince myself that the idea would work. If I stayed there, I'd be eaten. No question. It was just a matter of time. If I tried to escape, I could slip and fall to my death. So be it. That was still better than life here. Better than going berserk.

Then there was my arm. If the bird didn't kill me, my infected arm would. I had begun to notice that my arm had grown hot, and it was even more swollen and tender than ever. It had even wakened me out of a deep sleep several times lately. Severe pain now extended right up to my shoulder and into my neck. If I didn't get help soon, my wounds would kill me for sure. I tried to imagine what a slow, painful death from infection would be like. No! I had to escape somehow. I needed to get back to civilization. I needed a doctor.

I cracked my knuckles and stood up. Okay. Problema uno. How did I climb down a mountain I'd never seen? Surely there was a way down that wouldn't kill me.

I suspected, from the echoes, that a huge canyon lay below. I would have to feel my way down. Crawling across the huge nest, I extended my arm over the edge. The nest seemed to be resting on a flat rock. I felt my way around the nest, reaching over the side as I went. Near as I could tell, a wide rim of level rock lay outside the nest all the way around.

When I made the circle a second time, I noticed that the wind was stiffest on one particular side.

"Okay, that's got to be the side closest to the edge of the cliff," I muttered. To mark it, I found a good sized rock to wedge into the twigs of the nest on that side. "Now I'll know, when I feel that rock, that this is a danger spot," I muttered. "Don't want to get out of the nest on that side."

Then, I groped for the other three sides. Opposite the rock marker, on the far side of the nest, there was a rock wall just a foot away. No escape there. On the other two sides, the ledge felt much wider, so wide, in fact, that I could not reach the edge on either side.

Decision time. Should I leave the nest and go see how far out the ledge stretched? Which side should I start with? I decided to go to the closest side. I climbed out and reached my arms as far out as they would go. I still could not find an edge. I broke off a stick from the nest to use as an extension of my arm. By tapping the nest with the stick, I could reach out another two feet. I felt around and at last touched a rocky lip. There had to be at least five feet between the nest and the edge on this side. Beyond that, there was nothing. Just air. I found a small pebble and tossed it into the emptiness. It glanced off the rocks below for a full minute before the noise faded to nothing. I went weak at the knees. Just as I thought. I was a long way up.

I climbed back into the nest and crawled to the opposite side. Hauling myself out onto the rocky platform I again threw out my arms in a wide sweep, always using my stick to stay touching the nest. The ledge was even wider on this side. Even with my guide stick, I couldn't extend my arm far enough.

Then, all of a sudden, the sound of a loud crack ripped through the rock where I lay. Everything beneath me began to lurch and I slid backward.

"No-o-o!" I screamed and lunged toward the nest. It wasn't there!

"The nest! Where's the nest!" I yelled.

As I slipped back more and more, I thrust my arms out to find something to break my fall. I grabbed a bush—but a sharp pain shot through my hand.

"Ah-eey! Thorns!" I howled. But I didn't dare let go. I had to hang on. A few seconds later, the entire ledge gave away under me. I found myself dangling in mid-air listening to the rumble of boulders pounding their way to the canyon floor below.

The only thing standing between me and certain death was the tiny sticker bush. To let go was certain death. I thought about trying to pull myself up. Nope. Too risky. The roots of the little bush might give way. As the wind whistled around me and the cold seeped through me, my arm began to go numb. I still hung on. Again, I came face to face with my disastrous life. Helpless to change it I also knew nobody could save me now. I even took to praying.

"Oh God, if you're out there, I need your help."

That's when I heard the rhythmic *lop, lop, lop* of bird wings. Okay. Yeah. I was actually glad to hear it. When the bird swooped in, I felt my jacket tighten again as the creature hauled me up over the edge of the rock and dragged me back into the nest. I lay there gasping for air, my heart threatening to break my rib cage.

But the bird seemed restless. It began circling around me. The nest creaked and felt the long tail brush my face.

Then, without warning, the bird grabbed my arm—my wounded arm—and began tearing away at the jacket sleeve covering it! I tried to pull my arm away but the bird's weight pinned me down.

I gasped. "I knew it," I ground out through gritted teeth. In my panic I kicked like a wild man shouting, "Okay, you sicko wherever you are! I know you can hear me. I know you've got a video camera trained on this nest. Call off your flying dinosaur. Bet you forgot to feed it today, didn't you?"

"Get off me!" I shrieked and tried to pull my arm out from under the wicked talons. Between my screaming and my sobs I struck out with my other hand trying to free my arm.

"Barry, would you please hold still!"

I blinked.

Was that a voice?

CHAPTER 24: THE BIRD

*Though the facts may seem overwhelming,
believing the unbelievable demands character and courage."*
~Martin Moonglow

I froze. Was my mind playing tricks on me?

"That's much better. Thank you," said the strange voice.

I *had* heard a voice! "Wha . . . who is that?" I stammered, hardly daring to breathe.

"It's your friendly neighborhood bird of paradise. Now hold still," the voice said.

No way. That was too much of a stretch. This bird had to be little more than a trained monkey, at the whim of some bird trainer working out of a garage. No doubt there was a sadist out there somewhere with a remotely operated video camera pointed at us. I lashed out again at the bird's claw gripping my arm.

"I'll bet this is just a cruel gag!" I shouted, hoping I sounded braver than I felt. "You're some guy who's piped his voice into this nest for a cruel joke. You've trained this bird, haven't you?"

The ripping stopped.

"Believe what you like," the voice said, "But if I don't remove that worm lodged inside your arm, it's going to kill you.

Once it reaches your heart, your life will end. Now take off your jacket."

"No!" I shrieked. I was sure that I was talking to someone at the other end of a speaker wire. "This bird is trying to eat me!" I shouted. "Whoever you are, this has gone far enough!"

"All right. Have it your way," said the voice, and I felt the claw release my arm.

For a moment, I just lay there, stunned. My arm throbbed from all that wrenching and twisting. I rolled to one side and let out a choked sob.

"Why is this happening to me? Where am I? I want to go home!!" I howled. The canyon echoed back, "Home . . . home . . . home . . . ho . . . ."

There was a moment of silence.

Then the voice said, "I didn't think you ever wanted to go home again after what happened over your bicycle."

I stiffened and some bell went off in my head. "How . . . how do you know about my bike?" I asked.

The voice answered, "Barry, I know everything about you. Now take off your jacket."

I began to blubber like a two year old. "No! You want to eat me! I know it!" I cried.

"Stop that caterwauling, young man, and listen to me!" said the voice.

I stopped.

"Okay," I said, wiping my nose with my good hand. "I'm listening."

The voice began by saying, "Hasn't it occurred to you that if I had been planning to eat you, that I would have done it long ago?"

"Well . . . yeah, I guess," I said, snuffling.

The voice went on, "And haven't I fed you, watered you, and kept you warm all this time?"

"I suppose so." I hated to admit it, but I knew the bird was right. It was a question that had bugged me more times than I could count.

"Then why can't you trust me? Use your head, boy!" said the voice.

I couldn't speak. My brain was on overload. *Yo, Mr. Whoever-You-Are. It's hard enough to trust somebody when I can see him. Being blind makes it impossible.*

I flopped down on the bottom of the nest. "What choice do I have?" I asked.

"None," replied the voice.

I lay there breathing hard.

The voice went on. "On the other hand, I have several choices."

I moaned and ran my hand through my hair.

"First choice," the voice began, "We could continue as we were, and that worm in there will eat your heart out in a week. Two, I could just leave you up here to freeze. You'll be dead in even less time. If you want the truth, I'm leaning more toward this one every minute. If I don't see some respect and trust from you, I've a good mind just to leave you here to rot. You deserve no better."

I kept silent for several seconds. Then, I finally managed to whisper, "And the last option?"

"The last option," said the voice "is that I dig that worm out so you can live."

That was when I knew for certain there was no hope for me.

"Go ahead and leave me," I cried. "My life is wasted anyway. What use am I to anybody? I'm blind. I can never go anywhere alone again. I'm stuck up in this nest, and if I try to get out of it, I'll fall into a canyon. If I can't do a thing for myself, what's the point of living? Some weird bird is the only thing keeping me alive. Why, I don't know. I'm a useless lump. You might as well put me out of my misery."

I let my body go slack. With a voice that sounded like two rocks rubbing together, I muttered, "I give up."

After a brief silence, the twigs of the nest began to creak again. I just lay there, staring up into the blackness. The bird was moving around again, and I waited for it to fly away.

Then I felt something sting my eyes.

"Ow!" I yelled. Then I blinked. A burst of light filled my whole being. Like a black scarf lifted off my face, the darkness was gone. Oh, glorious light! I could see!

I looked up in wonder. There, standing right over me, was a magnificent creature. It's head was an iridescent purple with a feathery crown of yellow mixed with blue and its beak, at least two feet long, shone like real gold. The bird's piercing gaze was riveted on my face. And the stare – the stare was intense.

"Can you see me now, Barry?" the bird asked. *Incredible! The beak is moving. I'm face to face with a talking bird.* I managed a nod.

I sat up and looked around. My calculations had been pretty close. The bird's nest was sitting on a ledge high up on a mountain top. When I looked out over the edge of the nest, I swallowed hard. Below was a deep ravine with canyons veering off in several directions. From there, a sloping plain stretched out to the horizon. The nest itself was perched up so high that the rivers down on the plain looked like silvery ribbons on jade-colored velvet.

The bird spoke again.

"I wonder now if you would remove your jacket and let me look at your arm," it said. Without a word, I unzipped my jacket and slipped it off.

"Now take off your shirt and those dirty bandages," it instructed me. I complied, again in silence.

"Good. Now put your coat down on the floor of the nest and lie back on it," the bird said. I did as I was told and then stretched myself out still staring up at it.

"Barry, I won't lie to you," said the bird. "This is going to be painful, but it has to be done. Hold out your arm."

When I held out my swollen arm, I could see that not only was it swollen and turning purple, but . . . but . . .

"Aw-w!" I shrieked. "There's . . . there's something crawling under my skin!"

I started to go berserk again, but, in an instant, the bird had forced my arm down with one massive talon. It wasted no time. Using its razor-sharp beak, it made an incision the full length of my arm. I screamed and ground my teeth together. Then it went digging inside the wound. I nearly blacked out.

But in a matter of seconds, the bird found what it was looking for and started tugging. I could feel something coil inside my muscles. When the bird jerked hard a couple of times, a strange worm appeared above the incision clenched tight in the bird's beak. The creature was yellowish green, long and wiry, with purple blotches all over its back. It's mouth, crammed with rows of razor sharp teeth, gaped open. Hundreds of legs with crab-like pincers clawed the air.

I stared in horror. "What *is* that!" I yelled. "Get it away! Get it out of my arm!"

Then I made a decision. I rolled over sideways and, using my other hand, I grabbed onto the upper part of my lacerated arm. Every second felt like an hour.

"Quick!" I shrieked. "Take it out!"

The bird proceeded to play tug-o'-war with the creature. At first, the thing fought back, snagging the sinews of my arm like a night crawler holding onto a dirt clod. The bird continued to wrestle with it. Then, without warning, the worm let go with the snap of a live rubber band and latched onto the golden beak. Instantly, the bird lowered its head and tore the disgusting thing off with its talons, ripped it into chunks, and swallowed each piece one at a time.

It was the grossest thing I'd ever seen.

I looked down at my arm. Blood everywhere. *Uh-oh. I don't do blood.* Pain shot through my whole body and I suddenly felt woozy.

"That was very brave of you, Barry," said the bird. "Now, do you think you have enough strength to climb onto my back?"

Strength? I could barely talk.

"No," I whispered.

"Lie still then. I'll be back in a moment." The bird launched out over the canyon. True to its word, it soon returned with a sponge in its beak.

"Here, drink this, and drip some of it onto your arm," it said.

I took the sponge and drank my fill. The liquid was sweet. Then, as instructed, I squeezed the rest over my arm. Within seconds, the pain in my arm began to subside and I began to feel very sleepy. As I was drifting off, I felt the bird tucking the piles of downy feathers around me like Mom used to pull the bed covers up under my chin back home. I slept hard.

CHAPTER 25: SHOMARA

"Comparing death and life is like comparing black to white."
~Martin Moonglow

I woke to bright light and a blue sky. Though I had been sleeping without my shirt or my jacket, I wasn't cold. In fact, I was toasty warm. I turned my head. Next to me, with a wing stretched over me, sat the bird. It stirred and looked down at me.

"Good morning, Barry. How's the arm feeling?" he asked. I stared again at the golden beak. *That beak really moves when the bird talks. It even makes a clicking sound at the end of every word.*

I brushed away the feathery down and checked out my arm. I couldn't believe it. The incision had closed up while I slept. Still, the arm was twice the size of the other.

"Um, my arm's okay, I guess. It doesn't hurt. Just looks funny," I answered. *Criminy. I'm turning into Popeye, one arm at a time.*

"Can you get your shirt and jacket back on?" asked the bird.
"I think so," I said.
"I'm hungry. Are you ready to get off this mountain?" it asked.
"Totally," I said, sitting up. I grabbed for my clothes. Out of the corner of my eye I studied the great creature. If ever a thing embodied the theme of "living color," it was this bird, from the

purple and gold feathers that crowned his head down to the fluorescent blue-green plumes that cloaked his huge talons. Reds, oranges, purples, and greens all shimmered and rippled in the light whenever the bird moved. It stood at least twelve feet high with a wing span of around thirty feet. But its tail! The tail drifted out behind it like an elegant, folded fan. Okay, yeah. The giant bird was spectacular.

I finished dressing while a dozen questions bubbled up inside me. At last my curiosity got the better of me. "So, do you have a name?" I blurted out, "Like something other than 'Bird of Paradise,' I mean. That's kind of a mouthful."

"Yes, Barry," replied the giant bird. "My name is Ayshwa. Now, are you ready for some roast chicken?"

"Ay—what?" I didn't think I'd heard right.

"Ay—sh—wah."

"Funky. But what's that you said about chicken?" I asked.

"Oh, chicken," said the bird. "I just wondered if you were ready for some chicken."

"Cooked?" I asked.

"Yes, barbequed no less," he answered. "Do you think you would be able to ride on my back? It's about the only way we're going to get you down, unless I claw you like I did the first time."

I looked up into the bird's piercing gaze. "I'd like to ride if you don't mind," I said. Just the thought of being a mouse again made me shudder.

He lowered a wing so I could climb up onto his back. But no sooner did I try to seat myself than . . . "Ah-h-h!" I slid off the other side and landed in the middle of the nest again.

The bird began a screech-caw. Now, if I hadn't known better, I'd have thought it was laughing.

"There's nothing to hold on to up there, uh . . . Ayshwa," I said as I unhooked myself from several twigs.

"Yes, I know," said Ayshwa. "I just love to watch kids try anyway. It's so funny when you slide off." At that, he started into more screech-cawing. So I was right. The bird *was* laughing!

When he settled down he said, "Now that I've had my fun, young Barry, climb onto my back and I'll show you a few things." I obliged, and was soon sitting on his back still feeling rather precarious. The bird went on. "Reach under my feathers in front of you now, right about where my wings join up with my torso," he said. I ran my hands under his feathers and found two boney grips that seemed to have been made just for my hands.

"Hey, there are some handles under here," I said.

"That's right. Now feel around with your feet just forward of my wings to find the stirrups."

After wiggling my feet around, I hit a couple of hard things and my feet slipped into stirrups. Then I felt movement as if they had just surrounded my ankles.

"Whoa! Did I just feel those stirrups wrap around my feet?" I asked.

"Yes, you did. Now check this out." Ayshwa spread his wings wide and, all of a sudden, a chair-like saddle rose up under me and wrapped itself around my waist.

"Yow! How do you do that?" I asked rocking back and forth in the new contraption."

"Do you like it?" asked the bird.

"Yeah, pretty cool," I said. "But how do you get stuff to grow right out of your body?"

"Oh, I'm no ordinary bird," said Ayshwa.

No bleepin' duh.

The bird continued. "Are you ready for your first test flight?" he asked.

"Okay by me. I'm game if you are!" *Wait. Did I say that out loud?*

Ayshwa hopped onto the edge of the nest. "Hang on, Barry! Showtime!" With that, the great wings stretched out over the canyon.

We first descended with such speed that my stomach was rammed up my throat. Then we hit an updraft and began soaring way up over the mountain peaks.

"Ya-hoo-oo!!" I shouted. "This totally *rocks!!*"

In contrast to my first harrowing flight, this one was exhilarating. For one thing, I could *see!* I had never appreciated my sight until that day. Now, my eyes could not get enough of the color around me – a pink morning sky and funny shaped clouds of blue and gold overhead. In one cloud, I was sure I saw my buddy, Chad, sticking his tongue out at me. And the foothills below! They looked like wrinkles on the Green Giant's face.

Then, up over the next hill, a vast patchwork quilt spread out below. As Ayshwa and I got closer I saw it was acres and acres of flowers and crops growing in squared off plots on the plain.

Chad would totally flip out if he saw this. Who am I kidding? I can hardly believe it myself! I mean, I was really trippin' – whipping up and down the air currents on the back of a bird! From now on, mere bike rides will be Boresville.

Ayshwa began to point out various landmarks to me.

"Do you see those mountains in the east straight ahead, Barry?" the bird shouted.

"Yeah," I yelled back.

"That's the boundaries of your inheritance. You are one of the famous princes of the realm you know."

I laughed. "Sure!" I shouted back. *. . . And my mom is the Queen of England.* Inheritance? The only inheritance I knew about was a stamp collection that my grandfather was saving for me. Gramps said it was worth several thousand dollars. He said he wanted me to use it to buy books and a decent computer when I went to college.

"Still hungry, Barry?" called Ayshwa.

"Famished!"

"I smell barbeque. Let's go see what we can find," yelled Ayshwa.

He went into a steep dive and I nearly lost my grip. I was glad his saddle held me secure. I leaned back until my body was nearly stretched flat on his back.

"Yee-haw! This is better than a roller coaster!" I squealed. He let out a shriek and brought both of us out of the dive, swooping so close to the ground that I could have plucked a dandelion. And I'm positive I left my stomach dangling from a tree limb.

Ayshwa came to rest on the top of a flat rock. "Breakfast time! Let's eat!" he said. He laid out several fully cooked chickens on the rock.

"Wow! This looks fabulous," I squealed. "But who prepared these? Won't the cooks be ticked off that we took their food?"

"Good question, Barry. It's actually the other way around. The people of this land always prepare more than they need. It's their fondest hope that I will enjoy some of their meal whenever I pass over their houses."

"Hm," I said. "That's weird. Where I come from, somebody would probably grab a shotgun and blast you out of the sky."

"Sounds like a sad place," he said. "Now eat as much as you want," he said and stepped back.

Ravenous, I stuffed myself while the bird kept watch. At first I thought it was odd that he would bring me chicken but then I remembered that hawks and eagles do eat other birds. But even as hungry as I was, I didn't make a dent in the half dozen chickens he had collected.

After I had eaten my fill, Ayshwa dove in and devoured the rest. No sooner had he finished his meal, than, bird-like, he began to preen all his feathers, straightening and smoothing them out.

The bird's behavior continued to weird me out. Why did he let me eat first, and serve himself last? To say that Ayshwa was an extraordinary member of the fowl family was an understatement.

This creature has saved my life several times over, fed me, watered me, and kept me warm for maybe weeks. I was blind and he gave me back my sight. Then he tore a gi-normous worm out of my arm and even gave me something for the pain. Now, this morning, he took me for the ride of my life and fed me breakfast . . . . I didn't get it.

I shook my head. A twelve foot bird was fantastic enough. A bird that had the human qualities of love and patience? That was more than my puny brain cells could handle.

With our stomachs full we took to the skies once more. A rich green valley opened up in front of us at the base of the foothills. Just beyond a grove of palm trees I spotted a body of water so blue it looked like a gem stone. It stretched to the horizon, waves lapping on a white sandy beach.

Hold it. *Palm trees?*

"Hey, where is this place?" I called to Ayshwa.

"Shomara!" he shouted back.

"What?"

"This is Shomara," repeated Ayshwa, dropping to the beach.

I scrambled out of the saddle, dropped to the sand, and ran around to face the bird. "Sorry. I didn't hear you," I said. "What did you say, Sho . . . ?"

"Shomara, Barry. Sho-MAR-ah," said the bird, preening his feathers again.

"I've never heard of it. How far is it from my grandfather's place?" I asked completely baffled now.

"Oh, a couple of galaxies, I'd say," said Ayshwa, ruffling his feathers.

"A couple of galax. . . !" My jaw dropped. "But . . . ?"

Ayshwa spoke. "Barry, it's like this. When you stepped through that carved wooden gate in your grandfather's backyard, you stepped onto Shomara, a separate planet that resembles earth but ever so much nicer, don't you think? I'm always finding folks coming through that gate."

I felt a wave of panic. "How long have I been here? I figure it's been at least three weeks. Will I ever be able to go back? Will I ever see my mom and my sister again?" I remembered movies about how space explorers had traveled to other worlds and because of some Einstein theory or whatever, they didn't age. But when they came back to earth, they found themselves in the future. All the people they had known were long dead.

Ayshwa laughed. "You have nothing to worry about. And it's not been weeks, Barry. Not even days. By earth time, you've been gone just a few minutes."

Again, I couldn't believe it. "No way!" I exclaimed.

"'Yes-way,' as you put it," said Ayshwa. "It's true. Our passage of time here is very different."

I walked across the beautiful white sand. Whew! It sure was warm here. I dropped my jacket onto the beach and reached down to let the waves wash over my hands. Now I knew why I hadn't seen any houses from the neighbor's backyard. This wasn't anyone's backyard. I was on a different world, in a different realm altogether. That gate must be something like a wormhole through space!

I turned around.

"So will I ever be able to go back? I mean, could I maybe still make it to school on time?" I asked.

"Of course," said Ayshwa.

I hesitated and then sat down on the beach. Staring out across the water, I scooped up handfuls of the white sand, letting it run through my fingers.

"Can I . . . uh, can I come back if I leave?" I asked, not daring to look at the bird.

"Anytime, Barry," Ayshwa answered.

I heaved a big sigh. "Can I bring a friend?" I asked.

"Yes, of course. If your friend can see the gate, he's more than welcome," Ayshwa replied.

"What do you mean?" I stared up at him.

Ayshwa shook his great head. "Folks can't find that gate unless they're ready for it. But I would be delighted to meet any friend of such a brave young man as you, Barry."

I stood up. Kicking a few pebbles at the edge of the beach, I cleared my throat.

"I don't know about the brave bit," I said. "I should be dead right now. I don't know where I'd be if you hadn't taken that worm out of my arm. I mean, I didn't even know it was there."

Ayshwa fluttered his wings. "Still, you let me do it, Barry," he said. "That was no small feat."

"Yeah. Well, I want to thank you anyway," I said. On an impulse, I made to hug the bird's leg. Ayshwa bent his head and I wrapped my arms around his neck and held him tight for a moment.

"Will you take my friend for a ride if I come back?" I asked. *Hey there, Barry Boy. Better watch it. You're pushin' the limits.*

"Certainly I will," Ayshwa said.

I looked up at him in surprise and shook my head. "You're awesome, you know that?" I said.

"I'm very glad you think so. Now, are you ready to get back to the gate?"

"Yeah, I guess," I said, feeling sad all of a sudden.

"Don't forget your jacket over there by the water," said Ayshwa.

"Oh, right. Thanks," I said. I ran over, got my jacket, and then climbed back up onto Ayshwa's back.

Ayshwa waited until I was secure, and then turned his head right around, bird fashion, to look me full in the face. *That has got to be the freakiest thing birds do.*

"What do you plan to do about the bicycle problem, Barry?" Ayshwa asked.

I stared at him and then looked away.

"I don't know yet," I said. "Oh, I know why my Mom is going to sell it, all right. I used the bike to disobey her. It's just . . . rats! It's gonna take me *years* to find another bike like that one!"

"Did you buy the bike, or did your parents buy it for you?" Ayshwa asked.

"I shopped around for it, but they bought it for me two Christmases ago."

Ayshwa paused. Then he asked, "Are you willing to do without your bike until you earn back the privilege?"

"How's that?"

"Well, perhaps your mother would agree to put your bicycle in storage until you earn the money to buy it from her."

I thought about that for a moment, and then nodded. "Maybe," I said. "She might. At least I can ask her. And . . . yeah! I could get a paper route or something." Funny. I felt much lighter all of a sudden.

"There you go!" said Ayshwa. "It's always hard to admit you've done something wrong. But there's usually a way to make things right. Ready to go now?"

"Yup!" I yelled. "All set. Let's slice a few clouds!"

Chapter 26: The Blood Jewel

"In Shomara, wealth is a living, breathing entity, always growing, always expanding."
~Martin Moonglow

As Ayshwa took to the air in one leap, I held onto the handle bones with all my might. The moment we rose above the palm trees an updraft found us. I couldn't help it. I squealed like a five-year-old. Soaring high above the sea, the bird made a wide turn to the left to follow the shoreline.

I leaned forward and laid my head on the bird's neck. The feathers were not what I expected. They were as soft as silk.

I lay there trying to take in the sights below me. The water glittered like a jewel and the beach—it looked like it was littered with diamonds. Hundreds of coconut palms fanned out across the green plains, flower bushes lined little streams everywhere (my mom would love that!) and acres of corn stretched as far as I could see. Hay bales, like giant bricks of gold, lay baking in the fields. And the fruit in the orchards? So many apples and pears hung from the trees that the branches sagged to the ground. In fact, I'd say 'Land o' Plenty' about covered it.

In no time, we flew over the large river I remembered from my first minutes on Shomara. I recognized the cliff where it ended and plunged into the basin below.

"There's a waterfall over there, and below it is a pool," I shouted. Sure enough, as Ayshwa rounded the bend of the next large hill, I saw the waterfall splashing out over the rocks.

"There it is," I shouted. "Grandpa's gate should be up on that hill over there," I called out.

"You're right. Hold on!" the bird shouted and began his descent to the plateau above the green pool. When Ayshwa settled and closed up his wings, the saddle disappeared and I slid to the ground. I glanced down at the pool one more time. *Strange. How could I have missed all those palm trees growing down there? Oh yeah. That was when I was hit by that flash of light.*

"Ayshwa," I began, "What was it that blinded me that first day I was here?"

The great bird studied me for a moment. "Perhaps it was a combination of the poison from the maggot, and your deep anger," said the bird. "Light tried to get in, but you wouldn't let it. There are many kinds of blindness, Barry."

"So what was it that you dropped into my eyes so I could see and how come you didn't do it sooner?" I asked.

"It's a secret Shomara potion, Barry, but for a while, you weren't ready for it," Ayshwa said. "I had to wait until you gave up struggling. I had to have your cooperation. I did not want to fight you and the maggot at the same time."

Oh," I mumbled. "Well . . . uh, I just hope it never happens again."

"It won't," said the bird. "In fact, I'm going to give you something to protect you from any more worm attacks."

I blinked. "Why would you do that? I mean, the truth is, I was stupid and that maggot found its mark. End of story," I said.

Ayshwa tossed his great head. "Be that as it may, this will prevent it ever happening again. There are many things planned for your future. I want you to be protected from these attacks so that you can accomplish your mission."

"Oh. Okay," I said. Then I looked up at him. "Mission? What mission?"

"Come closer, boy," said Ayshwa.

I edged forward.

"Good. Now lift up your shirt." I raised my shirt. At that, Ayshwa reached down with his beak and plucked a small object from beneath the golden feathers of his chest. It was a brilliant red object about the size of a sunflower seed. But though it sparkled in the sunlight like a delicate ruby, I saw the bird's blood dripping from it. Before I could back away, Ayshwa had thrust it into my chest just below the collar bone.

"Ah-h-gh!" I gasped. "That stings."

But then, I felt warm. A surge of energy swept throughout my entire body. All of a sudden I had the feeling I could do just about anything. I looked down at the spot where the jewel had entered. There was a slight bump, but no open wound.

"Wha . . . what just happened?" I asked.

Ayshwa said, "I have just given you a blood jewel, Barry. You now have my life energy flowing through your veins. It also means you're now a legitimate citizen of Shomara. You are no longer an earth person. The source of your energy and life flows from Shomara now."

"One thing I must caution you, however." He shook his great head and ruffled his feathers. "This blood jewel is very precious. Under no circumstances are you to sell it or let anyone take it away from you. This jewel is a seed growing inside of you and is now your very life. You'll die without it."

I stood there trying to take in what he was saying. "Er . . . right. I'll remember that." I felt the place where the blood jewel had gone in. "I guess I wouldn't know how to dig it out anyway. Thank you, Ayshwa. I'd better be going if I'm going to get to school on time."

"That's right. Let me know how your mother takes to the idea of you earning back your bike," said the bird.

"Sure," I said. I turned to leave and then looked back at this fantastical new friend one more time.

"Y'know, Ayshwa, no joke. You're one cool bird!" I said.

"And you're a very brave young man, Barry," said the bird, and took off toward the cliff.

"Until next time!" he called back.

Nobody is going to believe this. I headed for the clump of bushes concealing the gate and pushed aside the shrubs. There it was, the strange carved gate in the plain fencing . . . no wait! The fence as well as the gate on this side—the Shomara side—was carved just like the gate. It even had the same unusual animals and birds on it. I lifted the latch. The gate swung open without a single squeak this time. Did someone oil this gate in the time I was gone?

I stepped through into Grandpa's yard, and a cold winter wind slapped me in the face. Br-r! I threw my jacket on, zipped it up, and retrieved my backpack from behind the tool shed. Soon I was jaunting across my grandparents' back yard. I was halfway across the lawn when my grandmother stepped out onto the deck still dressed in her housecoat and holding her morning cup of tea.

"Barry! What on earth brings you over this way so early in the morning!" she called.

"Oh, uh . . . hi Grandma!" *This must look pretty crazy to her.* "Um . . . I thought I'd swing by on my way to school. Uh . . . er . . . I was wondering if you and Gramps might have some odd jobs I could do around your house to earn some money," I said.

"Well, we'll sure give it some thought, Barry. What did you have in mind?" asked Grams.

I shrugged. "Nothing in particular. You know I'll work hard at whatever you give me."

"Of course, Barry. You always put your back into everything you do," Grams said. "No worries about that." She took a sip of her tea. "You know, we just got some free firewood scraps from a contractor just the other day. Huge pile of the stuff. I'll bet your granddad would love some help pulling nails out of that wood. That's all he's been doing for two days. Kinda hard on his old arthritic hands."

"Sounds good, Grams. I'll talk to Mom and make sure it's all right with her. I'll call you after school today, okay?"

"That'll be fine, Barry."

"Hey Grams. Can you tell me what time it is?" She looked at her watch. "It's 7:25, Barry. Are you going to be late for school?"

"Naw! But can I come in and use the bathroom first?"

"Of course." Grams swung the back door open. I rushed up onto the deck and through the kitchen passing Grandpa as he sipped coffee from his favorite mug.

"Mornin' Gramps. Okay if I use your bathroom?"

"Sure, kiddo. Just leave your quarter on the back of the toilet," Gramps said and then he grinned at me.

I chuckled. Same ol' Gramps, same ol' line. Then, I remembered my nightmare on the Shomara mountain. Today I was glad some things never change.

A few minutes later, I sprinted down the sidewalk toward school.

"Hey there, Master Barry! Where are you going in such a hurry?" It was Martin. He appeared out of nowhere and started jogging beside me.

"I'm going to school. It's what I do this time of day." I kept running. No way did I want to be late.

"Somebody is looking for you," said Martin.

"Yeah?" I countered. "Well, I know for sure it wasn't you."

"Well, I'm sorry I made you unhappy, Master Barry, but I was told not to follow you," Martin said.

I stopped. "Is that so. Is that why you didn't come and rescue me from that bird?"

Martin looked puzzled. "Bird? What bird?"

"The bird that carried me off to its nest high on the mountain over in Shomara!" I said, staring back at Martin. Then I threw up my hands. "Ah! How would you know! You weren't even there!" I started running again.

Martin blinked. "Shomara? You saw Shomara?" *Is that amazement I hear in Martin's voice? Nah.*

"Yeah, I saw Shomara. No thanks to you, I might add!"

Martin loped along beside me in silence for a full minute. Again he said, "Somebody is looking for you."

"Okay. You said that before. Who?"

Just then, a car honked from the street.

"Hey, Barry!" Colonel Sorenson waved at me from the driver's side. "Can I give you a lift?"

I ran over to the car, panting to catch my breath. "Sure, Mr. Sorenson," I said. As I climbed into the passenger side and buckled myself in, I noticed that Martin had seeped through the rear car door and was making himself comfortable.

"You're out early this morning, sir," I said.

The colonel fidgeted with the steering wheel. "Have you seen Chad?" he asked and cleared his throat. "I need to talk to him. I was on my way to the school hoping he was with you, but some road work was tying up traffic. Had to take a detour."

"I arranged that," Martin said. I turned around to see Martin looking very pleased with himself. "The Majesty let me I put up the road block so the colonel would have to take this road instead."

The colonel, who couldn't tell any other conversation was going on, said, "Your mother told me you left early this morning. She thought you'd be at school by now."

"Yeah, well, it was too early to catch the bus, so I came over to my grandparents house for a while," I said. "You said you wanted to see Chad?"

The colonel seemed to be clamping and unclamping his jaw. Then he swallowed.

"Chad is missing," he said.

Chapter 27: Martin's Surprise

"We rarely comprehend what is important to us until we lose it."
                                                                ~Martin Moonglow

I stared at the colonel. "Chad's missing?" I passed my hand through my hair. "I don't get it."

Colonel Sorenson's eyes looked glassy. When he finally spoke, his voice sounded like sandpaper. "Chad never slept in his bed last night," he said. "And this morning, no one could find him." He sighed and edged the car forward into the traffic.

I massaged my tired eyes. "But, but you've been back for . . . ." *Hold on. How long ago was that? Shomara has messed up my sense of time.*

I decided on a different tack. "So . . . uh, when did you get home, sir?" I asked, trying to sound cool.

"Just yesterday," answered the colonel.

"So when did you last see him?" I queried.

Colonel Sorenson looked over at me and grunted. "That's what I like about you, Barry. You never give into wimpy handwringing. You get right down to business. I wish Chad had your level head."

"Well, uh . . . thanks, sir," I said, biting my lip. "My mom would disagree. She'll tell you that I get chicken livers like everybody else." I cleared my throat. "So, did . . . did Chad talk to you at all after you got home?"

"Talk!" growled the colonel. "The kid ranted and raved like a confounded lunatic! Get this: he says I'm a spy! *Me!* A colonel in the military for twenty-eight years."

I didn't know what to say. I could tell by the way the colonel was working his mouth that he was upset. I didn't dare tell him that Chad had eavesdropped on his cell phone.

Mr. Sorenson gripped the steering wheel so tightly his knuckles were white. "I hadn't been home for more than an hour when Chad came barreling into my study. Said he'd been doing some research and he was convinced I was a spy. I'm a career officer in the United States military! I don't know where he got his ideas, but there was no way I could change his mind. To be accused of treason by my own son! I wish he'd punched me in the chops instead."

The colonel glanced over at me. I felt my face flush. *I wonder if he knows that Chad wishes he had a different dad.*

The colonel glared at me. "Oh, I know. I've not been home a lot during Chad's growing up years. He's thrown that in my face often enough!" *Huh. The man is a mind-reader.*

Then the colonel went limp. His shoulders sagged and he sighed. "Where the kid got his flimsy piece of so-called 'evidence' is beyond me! In the face of my entire career as a soldier, this blows my mind!"

The colonel slapped the steering wheel and gritted his teeth. "Do you know what it's like to have someone you love flush your whole life down the toilet? My own son thinks I'm a spy!"

I was still at a loss for words. I couldn't understand why this huge man was so angry at being called a spy when his only son was missing. If this had been my dad . . . . I got a lump in my throat. If I had gone missing, Dad wouldn't care two beans about his career. No. My father would have been freaked out of his mind worrying about *me*.

The colonel seemed to be expecting me to say something.

"I don't think you're a spy, sir," I whispered.

The colonel sighed. "Thanks for the vote of confidence, Barry. I appreciate it. And I'm also glad you're Chad's friend. Maybe, if we ever find him, you can talk some sense into him."

When the car pulled up to the school, I got out and said, "Thanks for the ride, Mr. Sorenson. Would you like me to give you a call if I happen to see Chad today? I mean, he may decide to show up for class even though he didn't come home."

"I'd be very grateful if you'd do that," the colonel said. "His mother is worried sick." I nodded. Then I saw the look of panic in the colonel's eyes and it dawned on me. *His anger is just a cover up. He is just as wacked out about Chad as his wife.*

So Chad was gone. I wondered if there could be demons chasing him too and I felt a wave of dread sweep over me. Where could he have taken off to? Surely he wouldn't do something to hurt himself. What happened to that wonderful bubbly feeling with Ayshwa this morning? Gone. Had it been real at all? Right now, reality seemed cold and bleak.

I moved like a wind-up toy for the rest of the day. I could no more focus on school than a dead hamster on an exercise wheel. Somehow my body walked its way to each class but I don't remember a thing. I was one daffy droid all day.

Now, you have to know, Chad was not the type to skip school. Making good grades was too much a matter of pride. Kids who make straight A's just don't cut class. But right off, he didn't show up for PE class. But when he didn't even show up for computer class, I really got concerned. I mean, Chad lived for computer class.

Maybe he'd been kidnapped. Nope. Chad was too ornery. Pity anybody who tried to haul *him* away in a dark alley. And I could only hope he was too strong-willed to end his own life. He just had to be hiding out somewhere.

I ruled out the arcade. Too public. Besides, his folks would have checked there already. The mall was a possibility, but there again, with store clerks and video cameras everywhere, there was no place to hole up. Could he have found some secret place in his own house to stash himself? Nah. The Sorenson place was too modern. Very few nooks and crannies. No heavy pieces of furniture where a kid could hide. The architecture was also too open. Scratch that. He was definitely not hiding at his house.

But the inevitable thought hit me anyway. I gulped. Why had Chad been so torn up last night? In spite of everything, I knew he idolized his father. It didn't matter that the colonel had ignored him all these years. But now, maybe he couldn't bear the thought of his dad being a spy. Truth was, it was the first time I'd ever heard

Chad cry. It did something awful to my insides. Maybe . . . . *Oh, please God, tell me he's not lying at the bottom of some cliff someplace.*

"Master Barry, I know where Chad is." Martin's voice jolted me out of my stupor. I looked around. "Martin, where are you!" I whispered.

"Sitting on top your ear," said Martin. At first I was forced to stay quiet because the teacher was handing out an assignment. As she passed, I raised my hand and asked to be excused to the restroom. Once I got there, I checked the place thoroughly to make sure we were alone.

"All right, Martin. Come out here where I can see your face," I demanded. My keeper complied, looking a bit sheepish.

I came right to the point. "So tell me where Chad is, will you?"

Martin stood there looking dazed. "Look," I said, feeling a bit sorry for him. "I can't talk to you just anywhere. On this planet, if people see you talking to yourself, they think you're ready for the nut house. Some kids at this school think I'm already there."

"Sorry, Master Barry," Martin said. "You don't have to answer me, you know. You never have before. I'm quite used to it."

I threw up my hands. "Look," I said. "Do you know where Chad is or don't you? Out with it and make it snappy. I've got to get back to class before they send out a search party."

"Right-o. Well, I saw Master Chad's keeper in an odd place this morning. He was standing high on the east side of the mountain where the sun comes up. We're good friends, Chad's keeper and me, because you and Chad spend so much time together."

This guy really has a talent for bugging me.

Between clenched teeth I growled, "How come you didn't tell me this four hours ago?"

"Well, Master Barry, you didn't seem very happy with me today, so I thought I'd better keep my mouth shut," said Martin. "Every time I said something, you snapped at me like a crocodile."

"Aww-gh!" I whirled away from him and walked to the far end of the rest room. Then, for no reason, I thought of Ayshwa and a calm breeze swept through me. I took a deep breath.

"Okay, Martin. My bad. When you didn't show up to help me on Shomara with that scary bird, I felt so alone. I mean, I thought your number one job was to protect me. Guess I needed some time to sort out my feelings is all."

Then I snapped my fingers. "Hey, Martin, I didn't show you. Check this out." I pulled up my sleeve and showed Martin my arm. "It was the bird who took care of it."

"Marvelous, Master Barry. Your arm does look much better. Much better indeed!" exclaimed Martin.

Even I had to admit it looked a whole lot better. Still a bit puffy but my skin was back to its normal color and the deep cut had almost disappeared.

Then Martin cocked his head and asked, " . . . A bird, you say?"

"Yup!" I said lowering my sleeve. "A humongous bird, Godzilla the Peacock, only with an even longer tail and feathers like a rainbow. Very colorful, but . . . but . . . ." I paused. What was that Martin said . . . ? "Wait. Did you say Chad has a keeper?"

"Yes, Barry. Of course he has a keeper. Most children your age have keepers," he answered.

I looked at Martin with new eyes. "So, " I said, "How many keepers do you know?"

"Millions," he said with a shrug.

"How many keepers are here at this school?" I asked.

"Hundreds, I'd say," said Martin.

I scratched my head. "Then how come I can't see them? I rub shoulders with dozens of kids and grownups every day," I said.

"Same reason you couldn't see me these last few hours," said Martin. "We sit under a collar, or in an ear. Lots easier to stay with our charges and not trip over each other's feet. But we call back and forth all day long. School is a big party for us."

"So you say Chad is up on a mountain?" I queried.

"Yes, Master Barry. He's tucked away in the side of the mountain up there."

Then the light dawned. I slammed my fist into my hand.

"Of all the . . . ! Of course. Why didn't I think of it before? There's only one place that matches that description. Our old summer hideout! That's it!"

I jumped into the air and hooted in relief. I felt like I was floating. Chad was alive!

"Martin, I could kiss you. There's a cave inside the mountain up there. Chad and I discovered it one summer and we fixed up a room inside the cave. It was our favorite getaway when the weather was hot. We promised each other that we would never tell anyone about it. It's been our secret place for years. That has to be it. And Chad will be waiting for me, and only me. I'm the only one that knows where to look so I've got to bring him down off that mountain. It's going to be up to me."

"I know the cave, Barry," said Martin, nodding his head.

"Oh yeah. Duh. I keep forgetting. Hey, thanks, Martin."

I looked up at the clock. "Whoops. Gotta head back to class. Now all I have to do is find a way to get up to the cave before the day's out." I rushed out into the hall, Martin again hitching a ride in my ear. This time I knew he was there because my ear got itchy.

Then I remembered. I stopped in the middle of the hallway.

"Oh no!" I whispered. "I can't go anywhere after school. I'm supposed to go right home on the bus. If I don't show up, Mom will blow a gasket."

Chapter 28: Transportation Hangups

"In every life, someone comes along who shows us a side of ourselves we never knew we had."
~Martin Moonglow

"Criminy! How could I forget?" I moaned. "I'm grounded. No way is Mom going to let me off the hook to go cruisin' around looking for Chad."

Inside my ear, Martin said, "I'm sorry, Barry. I forgot about that part, too."

Then I slapped my forehead. "And wouldn't ya know, today is also the day I was supposed to help Gramps pull nails. Now what? The real zinger is that I don't have my bike anymore. If I hoof it up to the cave it's a two hour trek one way. I'd be lucky to get there before dark. Even if Chad is there, we'd both be stuck for the night. It's too dicey to climb that mountain in the dark. Even Chad says so. And if he isn't there, I'll be in that cave all alone for the night. I'm not doing that." I shuddered. *I've had more than my share of cold, lonely nights on a mountain.*

First I needed transportation. I went back to my sixth period class and scanned the classroom for someone who lived in that area, someone who rode the bus.

Lupita Sanchez. Yeah. She lived up close to the hideout. And as far out of town as her house was, she had to be a bus rider.

I was well acquainted with the Sanchez Orchards. Our family had spent lots of happy hours there gathering apples in the fall. Mr. Sanchez always remembered our names even though he only saw us a few times a year. I figured the cave was less than half a mile up the canyon from the Sanchez place.

As soon as class was over, I walked up behind her.

"Hey, Lupita! How's it goin'?" I said.

Lupita looked up at me in surprise and . . . and she smiled.

"Barry! Everything is fine! How 'bout you?" she said.

Without warning, my whole brain shut down. Really. I forgot everything I was going to say. All I could do was just stare at her. *She has dimples. I never knew she had dimples.*

A full fifteen seconds later Lupita raised her eyebrows. "You okay, Barry?" she asked.

I shook myself. "Um . . . uh, yeah. Fine. I'm just fine." *Barry, you dork head! She's gonna think you're two fries short of a Happy Meal.*

I cleared my throat. "Um, listen. I have a buddy who's staying up close to where you and your brother live. I was wondering, do you think your bus driver would let me take your bus up there so I could go visit him?"

Lupita checked me over from top to bottom. Then she grinned again. "Hank Peters, bus driver—he's pretty easy going. He might need your parents' phone number to call and check, but yeah. No problem."

I let out a long sigh. "Thanks, Lupita! I'll have to call my mom to get permission. Guess if you see me, you see me, and if you don't, you won't. Bye."

"Bye, Barry! Hope I see you later." Lupita smiled again showing those great dimples.

I waved and speed walked to my next class. *Hoo-boy. Rendered brainless by a couple of dimples. How did that happen?*

First of all, I had to convince Mom that I knew where Chad was. Second, I had to make my case that I was the only one that Chad would listen to right now. And third, I had to persuade Mom to let me go it alone. Hoo-boy. It was going to be a hard sell after my latest screw-up.

Wait. What if I could get the colonel to call my mom instead? Maybe he could convince her to let me go find Chad. That might work. Between classes I went to the school office and asked permission to use the phone. I dialed the Sorenson number.

"Hello, Lucy Sorenson speaking." It was Chad's mother.

"Uh . . . hi, Mrs. Sorenson. This is Barry," I said.

"Barry! Have you seen Chad?"

"Well, no ma'am," I said. "He didn't come to school. But, I think I know where he might be."

You could have heard her shout down in Arkansas. It was so loud that I had to pull the phone away from my ear. *Poor Mrs. Sorenson. What a blonde-haired smurf-brain.*

After she calmed down, I said, "Mrs. Sorenson, I need you to do me a favor and call my mom."

"Sure, Barry. I take it that you want me to make sure it's okay with her that you help us find Chad? I'd be glad to. I'm sure she won't object."

"Well, ma'am, not so fast. You see, I'm grounded."

"So . . . you want me soften her up, is that it?"

"Yeah, something like that."

"I'll do anything you want, Barry," she said, and I heard her voice catch. "Just . . . just . . . . Oh, Barry, bring our boy back!" She went silent and I could hear her sniff. "Tell you what, I'll give your mom a buzz right now," she said. "But I'm sure it will be okay. I can't believe you ever mess up."

I cleared my throat. "Oh yeah, well. It happens."

"So you know where Chad is? Do you want Chad's father to come pick you up and go with you?" asked Mrs. Sorenson in a fake cheery voice. *Poor lady. She's ready to slide over the edge.*

"Uh . . . no, ma'am. Chad and I promised that we would never tell anyone about this location. I need to do this alone. Right now, I may be the only one he trusts. But I think I can have him home before dark."

"Oh, Barry!" she said. She started crying again. "I'll call your mom right away."

"Thanks, Mrs. Sorenson. Er . . . I gotta go to class now. Bye."

"Barry." Martin was walking beside me now. "Please tell me you are not going up on the mountain this afternoon."

"Why?" I asked. "What's wrong? You know I have to talk Chad into coming home."

"Yes, Master Barry. But you'd best hurry and get him off that mountain before nightfall. That's a very dangerous place after dark. Mm-*muh*!" said Martin, shaking his head. I stopped and stared at him.

"Wait. Back up. You said 'the mountain gets dangerous after dark'? Just what's that supposed to mean?"

"It not just talk, Barry," Martin said. "There is a great evil growing up in those hills. Amelia and I have been watching wicked spirits moving in and out of it for days now. It's even worse at night. We don't know what's going on yet but we are convinced that it's not a safe place for you or Master Chad. Since you are my charge, I would prefer you stayed home where it's safe."

Without warning, I felt my blood turn cold. I knew Martin was not someone who invented horror stories. I knew he would never intentionally scare me. So why would he choose a time like this to tell me this mountain was evil? I swallowed hard.

"Look, Martin. I know all mountains can be dangerous. But I have to get Chad to come home. If there is evil up there, then he's in danger too. Besides, he's expecting me. Are you saying that I can't count on you to protect me? Are these bad spirits that powerful?"

Martin didn't answer for a moment. Then he said, "No Master Barry. I can always call for backup. And just so you know, I admire the loyalty you have for your friend. If you are determined to hike up there this late in the day, I will be there with you. I would just prefer you didn't, is all."

I continued walking back to class. "Well, thanks for the heads up but I have to go. I'll get there and back as soon as I can. If Chad knew what I know now—the stuff you've just told me—he wouldn't hesitate to do the same for me."

"It's your choice, Master Barry," Martin said. "It's my job to warn you, that's all."

Back in class, I drummed my fingers on my desk and scanned the clock for the nineteenth time. *I should have stayed on Shomara for another week. I was so happy there.*

For the rest of the afternoon I wrote and rewrote what I would say to Mom when I called her. *I sure hope Mrs. Sorenson can convince Mom to let me go.* I also had to call Grams. I made a face. I decided to call Grams first and give Mrs. Sorenson time to work her magic on Mom. Talking to Grams would be like eating chocolate pudding. Talking to Mom could be like swallowing straight jalapeno sauce.

At last the bell rang and I made a beeline for the office to get to the phone before two dozen other kids beat me to it. As luck would have it, I was second in line. I stood there shifting my weight back and forth from one leg to the other.

"So, are you coming on our bus today, Barry?" It was Lupita. I felt a jolt of heat shoot through my whole body.

I stared down at her and took a deep breath. "Don't know yet. Still have to call my mom. That is . . . ," I said raising my voice. "That is . . . if this little cretin in front of me here ever gets *off the phone . . . !*"

The boy turned around and tossed his head. "Buzz off!" he growled. When I rolled my eyes, the guy slammed the phone down and snarled, "Okay-y! I'm gone. Y'happy?" With that he stomped off.

Lupita thought the whole thing was funny and laughed. *She has a cute laugh.*

"You've got plenty of time," Lupita said. "Our bus is always the last to leave. My brother and I are going to get a pop. I'll bring you one if you like." She flashed me another of her brilliant smiles.

"Uh . . . sure. That'd be great," I said. "Make sure it's something loaded with sugar, okay?"

"Got it," she said and disappeared into the crowded hallway.

"What a sweet child," said Martin, now standing beside me in the line. "Her keeper says she's very proud of her."

"What is your point, Martin?" I asked.

His eyebrows flew up and he put on an innocent "Who, moi?" expression.

I smothered a snort. "Martin," I said. "Don't even go there."

I grabbed the phone and dialed my grandmother's house first. I had no trouble explaining that I would not be coming after school today, that I was going to help find Chad. Grandma was very sympathetic. "We'll keep you and your friend in our prayers, Barry. You take care, now," she said.

That was like stroking a kitten. Mom will be a dragon at the dentist. I dialed home and when Mom answered the phone, I felt like a bowling pin slammed by a ball of lead. Would Mom and I ever be friends again?

"Uh . . . M-Mom! Has Mrs. Sorenson called you yet?" I stuttered. I felt my skin trying to slide off my bones.

"Yes, Barry, she did," Mom answered, her voice crisp. Then there was silence. I waited, but Mom still did not respond.

I cleared my throat. "So . . . so . . . do I have permission to go find Chad?"

I heard Mom heave a long sigh. "I don't know, Barry," she said. "This is the very first day you're supposed to be home right after school, and already you're asking for a new privilege."

I saw my heart splatter on the floor.

"Mom, please. Chad could be in danger. I'm about the only person he'll let come near him right now. I'm pretty sure I know where he is. I've gotta try to talk him into coming home."

Mom didn't say anything for a full fifteen seconds and my hand grew clammy just holding the phone.

"Okay, son," she said, "But how do you plan to get around without your bike?"

"I can ride a school bus up there," I said. "The driver will call you to make sure it's okay."

"All right, Barry. Chad's mother is counting on you," said Mom and then she paused. "Son, you know I love you, don't you? "

My eyes stung and my throat tightened. "I know," I said. Then I whispered, "Thanks, Mom."

When I hung up the phone, I was so relieved I jumped a full foot into the air—and almost made Lupita drop the soda pop she was handing to me.

"Wah-hoh!" she hollered holding my drink high in the air. "You nearly got a coke bath there! I take it that you will be riding our bus?"

"Yup!" I said. I took a long chug from my drink. "Man, does that hit the spot! Thanks, Lupita."

The bus driver, Hank, was okay though his hand shake was like a vise grip. After he called my mom, he grinned real big and waved me on back.

"Whew!" I muttered. "That game almost went into overtime."

"Right you are," said Martin in my ear.

I went to sit next to Lupita. Again, for some unknown reason, I had trouble breathing.

CHAPTER 29: CRACK-UP!

"In a crisis, help often arrives when you least expect it."
~Martin Moonglow

    I didn't remember much of the bus trip. All I could do was stare, hypnotized by the cute little face next to me.
    But I do remember seeing Lupita's keeper, Pink. She sat on the top of the seat in front of us dressed in—get this—a gown made of real pink rose petals. No kidding. The petals actually grew right out of her arms and her neck and she smelled like—well, roses. Right from the get-go Martin struck up a conversation with her. He decided to hang upside down from the overhead bins so he could talk to her face to face. I guess that was better than him hollering from the top of my ear.
    I really wanted to get to know Lupita but with Martin and Pink chattering above and next to me—and me trying to *pretend* I didn't hear anything—it was like trying to carry on a conversation in the school cafeteria. And remember, I was not allowed to let anyone in the spirit world, even Pink, know that I could see them.
    To add to the noise, Lupita had dorky little brother, Salazar, who sat right in front of us. Every two minutes he would turn around and spout a knock-knock joke. We all laughed until our sides ached.
    But then the Sanchez Orchards came into view and the bus ride was over. Did a bank of clouds just block out the sun?

"We're here," announced Lupita. "Do you need a ride to your friend's house?"

"Naw. I know my way from here," I said. I was determined not to let her to see which direction I was going.

"Thanks for getting me a ride on your bus, Lupita." Then turning to her little brother, I said, "And Salazar, if I hear another knock-knock joke out of your mouth, you'd better be making a pile of money cuz I'm suing you for air pollution." We all shared another round of laughs.

As I turned to walk up the street, I stopped and called back, "Hey, Lupita, wait." She turned to look at me and I ran back to her.

"Do you suppose it would be okay if later, I brought my friend down to use your phone?" I asked. "There's no service in the place where he's staying."

"Sure! Anytime," Lupita said. "My folks won't mind a bit."

Woo-hoo! Got another smile.

"Thanks, then," I said. "You guys have been great!" I waved and started up the road. Out of the corner of my eye I watched to make sure the Sanchez kids were inside. Then I veered off and began plowing up the side of the mountain. I knew the way by heart. Chad and I had hiked this trail many times.

But today, I felt strange, almost alone. I'd never trekked up here knowing about the spirit world before.

"Martin, are you in my ear right now? You're awful quiet."

"Yes, Master Barry. I'm here. I was just reliving my conversation with Pink, is all."

"Oh, yeah. Lupita's keeper. Did she really have rose petals growing right out of her body, or did I just imagine that?"

Martin chuckled. "Oh, she is a real rose all right. So sweet in every way, don't you think?"

"Uh, yeah." I didn't want to tell Martin that I thought a rose "person" was kinda strange.

All of a sudden, I felt prickly, like something was watching me.

"Martin?"

"Yes, Master Barry."

"While you're tucked down in my ear thinking about Pink, I don't suppose you could do a bit of keeper stuff for me, could you?"

"Sure, Barry. What did you have in mind?"

I hesitated to tell Martin how creepy I was feeling but I finally said, "Well, you remember you told me that this mountain was flooding with evil spirits?"

"Yes, I remember."

"Well . . . um. You're watching out for them, right? I mean, my head doesn't block your view of anything does it?"

"No, Barry," Martin said with a snicker. "Sitting in your ear is like sitting in the best box seat at a big baseball stadium. I can see everything. I'm always watching out for you."

"Thanks—I think." *Did he just say my head was empty?*

As I climbed I decided that the best way to keep my mind off spirit trouble was to tell Martin all about my Shomara experience. When I got to the part about the great bird taking the maggot out of my arm, Martin forgot where he was sitting and let out a whistle so loud he nearly sheared off the top of my head.

"Yiheee!" I yelled, and grabbed for my ears.

"Oh, I'm very sorry, Barry! I forgot I was still in your ear. Have I ruined your eardrum?" he asked.

"No," I said, "But maybe you should pop out and walk beside me for a while."

Martin was Mr. Apology himself. "I'm very sorry, Master Barry." He sprang out and became the size of a normal man. Then, still intrigued by my story, he asked, "So, this bird of paradise dug that worm right out of your arm?"

I nodded. "Yeah. No anesthesia either. It hurt somethin' awful. I lost a lot of blood, and felt sick to my stomach. The bird flew off and got me something sweet to drink that took the pain away and made me sleepy. By the next morning, the cut had closed up, although I still look like Popeye."

"Who is Popeye?" Martin asked.

I snorted. *How do you explain a cartoon to a spirit?* "Oh, it's a funny-looking sailor picture on TV," I said.

"Oh yes, now I remember," said Martin. "You used to watch him when you were a little boy." I blinked and shook my head. "Of course. You watched all my cartoons right along with me, didn't you? You are full of surprises."

All of a sudden, Martin jumped right in front of me. "Master Barry," he said in a low voice, "I need to warn you. There are several boys behind that rocky ledge to your rear. One of them has been watching and pointing at you now for several minutes."

I swallowed hard. "Are there demons in any of these boys?" I asked.

"Yes, several, and they appear to be controlling a gang of boys about your age. They ran out of an old hut up there on a hill, the one we passed ten minutes ago," said Martin.

I felt my chest tighten.

"What does the boy look like?" I asked. "The one who's been watching me, I mean?"

"Let me see. He's a big boy—stocky—with a large, square jaw, and a squashy-looking nose," said Martin.

I groaned. "Super. That's Dave Dimmerwitz. Works out at the gym all the time. He's got the whole six-pack look but he's missing the little plastic thingie that holds it all together. About as sharp as a bowling ball."

"What do you want me to do, Master Barry?" asked Martin.

"We're lookin' at big trouble here, Martin," I said. "The guy hates me. Why I don't know. He heads up a gang of punks that hate me too. One of them is Calvin Lumpskin, the screwtail that attacked me at the arcade, the one that infected me with the worm."

Martin tossed his head. "Ah. That devil," he said. "As I see it, this whole gang has devil problems."

I looked around for cover. "Martin, I've got to disappear," I said. "He can't catch me out here in the open, he just can't." I started running up the mountain, dodging trees and rocks, stumbling and scraping my knees as I went. Okay, yeah. I live up to my name all the time—Barry Klutzy. That's me.

Then I had an idea. Ahead of me was a high bluff that overlooked the trail below. I scrambled up the side. When I reached the top, I walked over to the edge. From there, I could see the gang riding toward me on mountain mopeds. They were using a series of switch backs to make their way down the escarpment on the other side of the valley. In no time they emerged from the valley shrubbery gunning their engines right below the bluff.

"Pick up some dirt and throw it." Who said that? I looked around but saw no one. With a shrug I scooped up a handful of dirt and tossed it into the wind. Maybe some grit would blow into their eyes or mess up their intake valves.

What happened next caught me by surprise. In the blink of an eye, sheer chaos erupted. Motorcycles began crashing into trees. Others plowed into briar bushes. Riders screamed as the thorns ripped into their faces. Still others whipped around and slid sideways in the dust. Two bikers, trying to avoid a collision, veered off the trail and hurtled right off a cliff. Others rode headlong into boulders, catapulting their bikes high into the air. As the howling operators became separated from their bikes, they slammed into fellow gang members roaring in behind them.

It looked like a game of high stakes dominoes as a dozen vehicles and drivers collided. It was sheer pandemonium. I couldn't believe it. No one was left upright. All I could see was a heap of spinning wheels, smoking engines, and . . . and some very angry demons.

That's right. From the top of that rocky hogs back, I watched the bikers tear off their helmets. The grotesque monsters underneath shook me to the core. Some had warts, some were covered with hair, others looked slimy with either spots or stripes. Some of them stood upright while others crawled on all fours. One had a tail like a scorpion and so many legs it resembled a centipede. Others had huge horns and weird tumors growing not only out of their mouths and heads but from their appendages as well. Several faces sported pig-like noses and large fangs that jutted up from their lower jaws.

And gaudy. I had no idea that demons came in such ghastly colors, some red, others blue, purple, chartreuse, and even fushia.

True to their kind, they were all very angry. They roamed around groaning and cussing as they picked themselves up out of the dirt. They didn't know what hit them. A little bit of dirt and in ten seconds they are a pile of junk. The truth was, I didn't know what happened either. I had just pulled off a blitzkrieg and didn't have a clue how I did it. But you have to know, I was definitely relieved.

"Oo-yeah!" I squeaked, punching the air with my fist. Then, without warning, Dave Dimmerwitz appeared roaring full blast up the side of the bluff straight toward me.

"Dang, you rat! How could the dust have missed you? And you were the main target." I retreated to the back side of the bluff and slid down the slope. But the moment my feet hit the grass, I heard Dave's bike sputtering around the rock to meet me. I looked frantically for a place to hide.

Then from behind me, a large sweaty hand clamped over my mouth. A second hand wrenched my right arm behind my back. Then my feet got kicked out from under me and I was hauled behind a clump of bushes into darkness.

CHAPTER 30: THE HIDE-OUT

"Secrets between friends should remain just that: secrets"
~Martin Moonglow

I could neither move nor speak. Dazed, I listened to my captor's heavy breathing while the sound of the motor bike faded into the distance.

Then a muffled voice growled in my ear, "You should've come alone, Barry."

It was Chad. I recognized his voice in an instant. I struggled to get away but Chad's grip was strong. Then I remembered a move he taught me. I forced myself to go limp. The weight of my body broke his hold just long enough for me to roll forward and away from his grasp.

I leapt to my feet and backed away.

"Of all the . . . !" I choked out. "Of course I came alone, Dork-brain! What-a-ya take me for? How was I to know Dimmerwitz and his thugs were in the neighborhood?"

"That was Dimmerwitz?" He sounded surprised. "Well! Then I probably just saved your skinny hide. He's always had it in for you, hasn't he?"

I dusted myself off. "Yeah. But why do you always have to be so physical? You could have just whistled or something."

Chad kicked a rock. "Sorry, 'kay? I had to act quick. Didn't want to take any chances that the guy on the motorcycle would see where our cave was, that's all."

I looked around. "But this isn't our cave," I said. "Where are we?"

"It's a new entrance I just found," Chad said. "I was exploring it when I heard all that rumble from the bikers. I didn't know those guys were chasing you until I heard you yell. Follow me. I'll show you where it leads."

As I dusted myself off, Martin spoke in my ear. "Master Barry, that was impressive. How did you do that?"

I let Chad go ahead of me enough so that I could answer Martin. "I dunno," I whispered. "Pretty weird, huh? It's like that dust blinded them or something."

"More than just 'something,' Barry," said Martin. "That dust you tossed made something a whole lot bigger happen."

"Maybe," I said under my breath, "But here's the kicker. I *saw* the demons that controlled the gang. I mean, what's that all about?"

"We need to talk," said Martin.

"I know, but not right now, okay? Chad will think I've gone whoop-de-doo if he catches me talking to thin air," I whispered. I started to walk more quickly to keep Chad's flashlight beam in sight along the twisted passageway.

"True," said Martin. "We'll talk later."

Making my way along the tunnel, I saw a second light up ahead. It was the hideout cave. Today, Chad had a hurricane lamp burning in it. Somehow, entering from this new angle made the cave seem bigger, more open.

It was clear to me that Chad had put some thought into his stay up here. Besides the lamp, he had a small cooler with food and soda pop, a lawn chair recliner, a sleeping bag, extra blankets, even a pillow. His clothes were tucked into a carry-all in the corner. All would have looked quite homey if it hadn't been for the Glock 19 lying on a box near the door. The sight of the gun turned my stomach.

"Chad, what's going on? This is crazy!" I said.

"You'd do the same if you found out your dad was a spy," said Chad, his face sullen.

"Chad . . . ." I threw up my hands. "I can't believe you would ever use a gun on your dad."

"No, but I might on the guys that are with him."

I shook my head and sat down on a rock. "So, how much do you know about your father?"

"Enough."

"Right. So you know more about him than the military does, is that it?" I asked. I hated to pick a fight with my best friend, but I didn't know what else to do.

"The military doesn't know diddly-squat," muttered Chad.

"What level clearance does your dad have?" I queried.

"I dunno."

"You don't know!" I croaked. "Chad, even a non-military person like me knows that the rank of colonel in any unit must have a security clearance up the wazoo!"

"It doesn't matter," said Chad. "He's still a spy." Then he turned on me and shouted, "I can't live under the same roof with an enemy of the state!"

"Whoa, Chaddo! Why are you getting' sore at me?" I chided. I was so bummed out that I just sat there for a full minute. *Talk about enemies. You are your own worst enemy, Chad.*

Then I had an idea. "Look, Chad," I said, "Let's say, for the sake of argument, that your dad really is a spy. Mind you, I don't buy it for a minute, but let's think this through. If your father is a spy, shouldn't he be watched carefully? Shouldn't you get as close to him as you can so you can follow his every move?"

As Chad stared into the fireplace, he reminded me of a wadded up T-shirt. He took a deep breath and said. "I hardly ever see my dad. You know that. How can I follow his every move if I never see him?"

"You're smart, Buddy. You'll figure out a way."

"Yeah? Well, I feel like an idiot right now," he mumbled.

I rolled my eyes. *Yeah-huh. Chad the ignoramus—with a 4.0 average nearly every quarter.*

"Look," I said. "You'll bounce back. You've just had a big shock, is all."

Chad sat there sullenly. "If my dad really is a spy, I don't think I could stand it!"

"Look, Chad," I said. "You're not the first kid who suspects his dad is working on the wrong side of the law. But look around. You'll never find out one way or the other if you're holed up here in this mountain. Man, you don't even have a computer." Chad didn't answer. Then I added, "Chad, your country needs you. You're a wizard at surfing the web. You can find out all sorts of things. Your dad won't be able to hide everything from you forever. Sooner or later he'll make a mistake. Either way, you gotta get out and face it like a man."

Chad stood up and started pacing the cave, dust kicking up from his boots. "I guess you're right. But why did it have to be my own father?" I took a deep breath but this time I held my tongue. I didn't want to overplay my hand.

Chad stopped pacing and looked at me. "You got any bright ideas what I'm going to say to him?"

I thought for a minute then said, "Chad, secret agents have to play many roles in order to get information. In your case, you're just going to have to pretend to be an obedient son so your dad doesn't get suspicious. Think you can do that?"

He pulled at his lip several times, then nodded. "Yeah, I guess."

I looked around the cave. "I think we should just leave this stuff for another day. Maybe we can pack it out this weekend. We need to get off this mountain before the sun goes down."

"Yeah. You're right," he muttered.

With that decision behind him, Chad found his voice again. "Man, Barry, you wouldn't believe how creepy it was up here last night. It was really cold and . . . and all kinds of weird noises. Nothin' like our nights up here last summer."

I stared at Chad and, from my ear, Martin spoke. "That's what I mean, Master Barry. Something evil is afoot up here. You've got to get Chad off this mountain, and it needs to be right *now*."

"Okay, Martin," I answered in a low voice. "You lead the way."

Chapter 31: Out of the Frying Pan...

"There are times when a gift feels more like a liability."
                              ~Martin Moonglow

We plunged down the mountain not even trying to stay on the trail. We had long discovered that by sliding down embankments and slicing across the switch backs we could cut our descent time in half. So in no time we emerged onto the road. I ran ahead to Lupita's house, hopped up the steps, and knocked on the door. Mr. Sanchez answered it.

"Yes? May I help you?" he asked.

"Yes, sir. My name is Barry Klutzenheimer and this is Chad Sorenson. We go to school with Lupita. We were wondering if we could use your phone for a few minutes."

"Sure t'ing! I 'member you, Barry," said Mr. Sanchez, beaming. "B'ery sad to hear about your papa. Use the phone? Si! No problema! Lupita, she tell me you might come by sometime. Come in, come in!" He waved us inside.

We were greeted by two dogs, three cats, and a wonderful aroma coming from the kitchen.

Lupita ran into the room. "Hi Barry!" she said with her bright smile. Nodding to Chad she added, "Right this way. The telephone is in the kitchen."

When I saw steaming food on the table, I realized that we had interrupted the family dinner hour.

"Oh. Sorry to bother you at meal time," I said. "As soon as we make this call we'll be out of your hair."

Lupita went over to a little round woman standing by the kitchen counter. "Barry, this is my mom," she said. "She doesn't speak a lot of English, but she's the best enchilada cook in the world. You should try some!"

"Well, thank you," I said, "I need to make this phone call first, though. Okay?"

I dialed Chad's home number and Colonel Sorenson answered. "Mr. Sorenson? Chad's here and he's ready to come home now." The colonel asked for the address, and hung up in less than thirty seconds.

Lupita repeated her invitation. "Come on and eat dinner with us," she said. "There are lots of enchiladas. My mom always cooks for an army."

Out of the corner of my eye I could see Chad drooling over the delicious smelling food.

"Well, if you're sure your folks don't mind," I said.

"I'm positive. We're used to lots of people around the table. In my family, we always have a couple of cousins or uncles staying with us at least half the year. I don't think my mom knows how to cook for less than ten." She laughed. At that moment, Mr. Sanchez came into the kitchen and waved us to take a seat.

"Sit, sit! We eat, si?" When Chad and I pulled our chairs up the dining table, Mr. Sanchez smiled with satisfaction.

"I'm afraid we don't have a lot of time," I said. "Chad's father is coming to pick us up in about fifteen minutes."

"That's plenty time to have at least four enchiladas!" Lupita said, sitting across from me. Again, I found myself staring at her. I was so deep in la-la-land that I almost stuck my finger into the enchilada dish.

A wave of panic swept over me. *I gotta get out of here! This girl is turning me into a total goofball.*

But the enchiladas were heavenly. The truth was, we were famished. I had worked up an appetite after my harrowing experience that afternoon and Chad—Chad was just plain hungry.

"I've decided I'm a lousy cook," he whispered to me. We grinned at each other. It was good to be enjoying a meal as friends again. But when a horn honked from out on the street, I looked over at Chad. His fork was frozen in mid-air, his eyes glassy. *Good grief, Chad, you are really messed up.*

I squeezed his arm then pushed myself away from the table.

"Thank you for the enchiladas, Mrs. Sanchez," I said as I stood up. "They were super good." I grinned using what I hoped was my killer smile. "I hope you will excuse us," I said to Lupita. "That'll be Chad's father so we have to go. Enjoyed seeing you, again, Mr. Sanchez," I said. *And your daughter.*

Chad and I walked out to the car where Colonel Sorenson was waiting. Chad tried to get me to sit in the front seat, but I shook my head.

"Remember. Face it like a man," I whispered.

"Yeah, right," Chad muttered. "Captain America. That's me."

We settled into our seats expecting immediate words from the colonel but he was quiet for several minutes. After taking the car out onto the highway, he said, "Good to have you back, son. You gave us quite a scare."

Chad gulped. "I know, sir. Sorry."

There was more silence. Then the colonel spoke again.

"Still think I'm a spy, Chad?" he asked.

Chad stared straight ahead. "I don't know, sir."

The colonel nodded his head. "That's a start." Then as much to me as to Chad, he asked, "Are you boys hungry?"

"We just ate some enchiladas at the Sanchez house," I answered.

Colonel Sorenson caught my eye in the rear view mirror. "Does that mean that you don't even have room for ice cream?"

I grinned. "I don't know about Chad, but I'm always ready for ice cream!"

With that, the colonel pulled into the closest dairy freeze shop. In no time, all three of us were tucking into hot fudge sundaes.

The conversation was bland for a while, until the Colonel asked, "You boys going to tell me where Chad's been holed up all this time? Your mom was fit to be tied, son. You know how strung out she gets."

Chad looked over at me and back to his father. Pursing his lips, he shook his head. "We can't tell you sir," he managed to squeak out.

The colonel studied him for a minute. Then he nodded. "All right. I can accept that. I can give you the benefit of the doubt there. In return, though, you might consider granting your old man the same favor." I noted that Chad kept his eyes down.

The colonel went on. "Chad, there are many things about my job that I cannot tell anyone. It's as much for your safety as it is for the security of my men carrying out the missions. The less you know the better. We all need to show some trust, don't we?"

I watched Chad meet his father's eyes for a brief moment. His wistful look tore at my gut. When we reached Chad's house, his mother rushed out to wrap him in her arms. I knew he must be embarrassed with me standing nearby.

Then Mrs. Sorenson came over and gave me a big mushy hug too. "Oh, Barry! I can't thank you enough! You brought my boy back!" I caught Chad watching me with sucked in cheeks and I felt my face go hot. I rolled my eyes. *He's wiggling his eyebrows at me, the renegade! I'll pound him for this.*

"Now you boys come on in," Mrs. Sorenson said. "We have a visitor that Chad will remember from Hawaii. We just found out that his mother is a professor here at the same university where Barry's dear father taught, God rest his soul."

About the time we entered the family's living room, my keeper, Martin, began talking really loud inside my ear. "Master Barry, just remember that evil spirits cannot read your mind. Keep that smile on your face at all costs." I wiggled my finger inside my ear. *Martin, you can be such a busybody at times.*

When we entered the family room, Chad's face lit up like a Christmas tree. "Daniel! How'd you get here!" he exclaimed.

A tall man strode over to Chad. He wore a multicolored shirt—obviously from Hawaii—open at the neck and khaki slacks neatly pressed. His hairstyle was the bed-head look with a slight Mohawk upsweep. With his cool, expensive looking watch he looked like he stepped out of a catalog. Add his bronze skin and handsome rock-star face and he reminded me of a walking, talking mannequin.

"Oh, I just stopped by to see my mom on my way to New York. Then I remembered that your family lived here in the same city."

"Barry, come over here!" said Chad. "This is Daniel Marek, the neat guy we met in Hawaii. Daniel, this is my best friend, Barry

Klutzenheimer. So, did you bring your wine colored BMW back with you?"

"Nope," said the man. "Too much trouble to transport. When I got stateside, I just bought a new one. It's the same color, but a newer model." Turning to me he said, "What did you say your name was?"

"Barry. Barry Klutzenheimer," I said.

"No kidding? I knew a dude in high school named Barry. Super name," he said, reaching his hand out to me.

"Thanks," I said.

But when I took Daniel's hand, I found myself clutching instead . . . a massive dragon claw!

CHAPTER 32: DANGER IN DISGUISE

"Fear sets in when we have only ourselves to trust."
~Martin Moonglow

I stiffened, still holding the claw. Little by little I lifted my head to see what the claw was attached to and found myself face to face with a giant screwtail. It was far bigger than the one at the arcade. This one completely filled Daniel's space—claws attached to fat greenish grey arms, a thick, scale-covered body, massive bald head, drooling mouth, jagged teeth, and a spiked tail that lay like a wicked slug behind him.

Inside my ear, Martin kept whispering, "Just keep that smile in place, Barry. Keep smiling. You're doing just fine. Just fine. No sudden actions now. That's the key. Just pull your hand away a little at a time . . . that's it, that's it."

I forced my hand to make slow, deliberate moves as I let go of the claw. Only then could I bring my hand down to my side. The moment I let go, Daniel's normal face came back into view. I tried to brace myself so my face didn't give me away.

I didn't do so well. Daniel had been watching me. He smirked, "You okay, kid? You look like you've just seen a ghost."

All I could say was, "Er . . . it's just that you remind me of a guy I saw down at the mall last week. He could be your twin."

Martin burst out laughing. "Oh that was good, Master Barry! *Very* good, indeed!" As for me, I was surprised I was still on my feet, let alone able to talk a complete sentence.

Just then, Chad's sister, Kayla, came into the room. She, too, was all gaga over Daniel. What a non-stop giggler. She always made me want to yank the skin up around my ears. With Daniel in the room, her giggle-ometer had spiked nine notches. She made me want to shrink into a knot.

As I watched the family hover around Daniel, I could not shake a heavy sense of foreboding. Then I realized something. I was the only one who knew who Daniel really was!

What could I do? I couldn't run up and accuse the man of anything because, in the eyes of the law, he had done nothing wrong. But there was no question. Daniel was infested with a screwtail. That meant Chad's family was in real danger.

For the hundredth time, I wished I didn't have spirit sight. What was the point of this so-called "gift" anyway? I couldn't tell a soul. Who would believe me even if I did? Everybody would dismiss me as a total nut job. The reputation as "Brainy Barry" was bad enough, but Barry Bonkers? Nope. But there had to be some other way to help the Sorensons.

I felt so helpless. *I need to get away and think.*

I went over to the colonel. "Um . . . Mr. Sorenson, do you mind if I use your phone?" I asked. "My mom is going to wonder if I dropped off Planet Earth."

"Of course, Barry. You go right ahead," said the colonel. Taking me aside, he added, "As far as I'm concerned, young man, you can use anything in this house you want. You've done us a real service. I can't thank you enough."

"You're welcome, sir," I said. A warm glow filled my insides. *Wow. Feels good to be appreciated.* I found the phone and dialed home.

"Sylvia Klutzenheimer speaking."

"Hi, Mom. It's Barry. Can you come over to Chad's house and pick me up?" I asked.

"Sure, son. Did you find Chad?" asked Mom.

"Yup. He's back, safe and sound."

"Did he come home by himself?"

"No. I had to do some pretty fast talking there for a while."

"Well, good for you, son. I'm proud of you." For the second time in the space of a mere two minutes, I felt good about myself.

"I'll be over just as soon as I can," Mom said. "Jenny says to tell you she's proud of you, too." I grinned to myself. *Cool. Triple whammy. I should do this more often.*

I went back into the living room and sat down in a corner to watch Daniel. Even if I hadn't known he was a screwtail, I could see why the guy made the colonel nervous.

He was too smooth, like a radio talk show host. He could bat his gums about anything. I gulped. *The only chink in his armor is me. I know who he is.*

I knew I had to do something. If I didn't, the Sorensons were sitting ducks. *But I'm only a twelve year old nobody. How can I even pretend to take this guy on? He's rich, good looking, and acts like he's got the whole world by the tail. He's invincible.*

I sat there mulling over this new dilemma while my enchiladas churned inside my stomach like so much molten lava. They had tasted so good going down, but now, in the face of this crisis, they were threatening to come back up. I was glad when Mom drove in and I could escape to her car.

Colonel Sorenson followed me out. "You've got a fine boy here, Sylvia," he said. "If it hadn't been for him, Chad would still be out there somewhere. Thanks for loaning him to us."

My mom was all sweetness and sugar. "Glad to help, Max," she said. "Your Chad has always been a good friend for Barry. We're happy everything turned out okay."

"I hear you and Lucy had a great talk this afternoon," said the colonel.

Crud. There goes my good mood kablooey right out the window. If I know Mom—and I do—that 'talk' was probably "fried-Barry-on-rye."

Back home, my mom gave me a big hug and told me again that she was very proud of me. Then I felt guilty. Okay, so why did I assume that Mom would air my dirty laundry with Mrs. Sorenson? I just told Chad a few hours ago to give his dad the benefit of the doubt. Maybe I should pop a few pills from my own medicine cabinet.

All of a sudden, I was exhausted. It seemed like forever since I'd been in my own bed. I longed for the smell of clean sheets and the feel of a soft pillow. *Bird's nests are made for . . . well, birds.*

"Master Barry, you did very well today," said Martin as we headed for the bedroom. "You stopped those demons out on the mountain side. You talked Chad out of staying in that cave another night. You helped him mend the rift between him and his father. And you even stayed calm in the face of that screwtail. You have had an amazing day."

"Thanks, Martin," I said as I wriggled out of my clothes.

The keeper cleared his throat. "But now, I have a question for you."

I yawned and flopped down on my bed. My eyelids felt like they were made of lead.

"Yeah? What's that?" I mumbled.

"Do you have any idea what happened with the bike gang this afternoon?" Martin asked.

I shrugged and plumped up my pillow. "Nope," I said, "I thought you knew. You've seen this before, right?"

Martin shook his head. "Not really. In all my millennia—and I've seen a great number of them—I have never seen this happen except when . . . ." He paused. "Master Barry, did that giant bird give you anything before you left Shomara, a token, a bit of something to remember him by?"

I heaved a sigh, and sat up. "Well, yeah, he did, come to think of it," I said and yawned again. I pulled up my pajama top. "Ayshwa pulled this little sparkly thingy out of his chest and stuck it here right below my collar bone. See that?" I ran my finger over a slight bulge under the skin of my chest. "You can feel the little pokie end of it just under the surface. I forgot all about it."

I looked over at Martin and was surprised to see him sitting on the nightstand staring off into space. Almost to himself my keeper whispered, "A blood jewel."

"So, what's that got to do with today?" I asked.

"Everything," said Martin nodding his head. "So that's what the Majesty was hinting at when he said he was accelerating your learning so that you were ready. I'm sure it has something to do with the mission."

"Ready for what?" I asked.

"To quote you, Barry, 'I don't have a clue'," Martin said. "The Majesty spoke of a mission. I suspect giving you this blood jewel plays a major part in it. We may not know all the ins and outs of it yet, but this we can be assured: the Great One is in charge and he is good."

"Well," I mumbled, "I'm just glad that I didn't have to face down those ugly creatures in that bike gang. I've got enough to deal with without that crowd."

Then a flash alert hit my brain. I sat straight up. "Martin! What am I going to do about that screwtail today, the one at Chad's house? The Sorenson family is in danger but I can't tell them."

Martin blinked. "What do you mean, Master Barry?"

"Daniel Marek. We both know he's AAD—armed and dangerous. Trouble is, the Sorensons all think the guy hung the moon. Well, okay. The colonel doesn't but the rest of them do. They would never believe he's a criminal. What'll I do? I just can't stand by and watch him hurt Chad's family," I said.

"I wish I had an answer for you, Barry," Martin said. "This is a real cucumber, for sure."

"Cucumber? Cucumber . . . ." I stared at Martin. Then I threw myself back on my bed in a laughing fit. I laughed so hard I was gasping for air.

At last I blurted out, "Oh Martin. I needed that!"

"So what did I say that was so funny?" he asked.

I roared again. "You said . . . *(snort)* . . . you said, 'cucumber.' I know you meant 'pickle' but it's *so funny* when you butcher the English language."

"Oh. Cucumber and pickle are not the same?" asked Martin.

"Nope," I said still holding my stomach. Then I sobered a bit. "You don't mind when I laugh at you, do you?" I asked. "Chad and I make fun of each other all the time. It's what friends do."

Martin grinned. "It's fine, Barry. It's not like I haven't poked fun at you a time or two. I'm just glad you enjoy having me around again, especially after I didn't help you on Shomara."

I nodded. Okay, one more yawn. "Well, if you weren't allowed to follow me as you say, then I don't hold it against you. In spite of everything, you're turning out to be a real friend. 'Night, Martin," I mumbled and pulled the covers up.

My keeper smiled. "Goodnight, Master Barry."

Martin didn't know it, but just as I was closing my eyes, I saw him punch the air with both fists and mouth a silent "Yes!"

EPILOGUE

When Martin entered the courts of the Majesty soon thereafter, the Great One called him forward.

"Well, Martin, tell me. Have you figured out what the mission is yet?" he asked.

Martin bowed and nodded his head. "I believe, Your Majesty, that it must have something to do with protecting the Sorenson family from that screwtail. Am I close?"

The Great One laughed. "Oh that is just the tip of the iceberg, my dear keeper. There is so much more to it than that. When you do finally figure it out, you are going to love it."

"So does that mean you are not going to tell me anything more?" asked Martin. "Must I still work in the dark?"

"Oh, we never use the word 'dark' around here, Martin," said the Great One. "Nothing around here is dark to me. I see everything. I even know what you are going to do before you do it. It's just that I love to surprise folks. It's so much fun."

"Surprising us is fun for you?" Martin queried.

"Of course," said the Majesty. "Don't you see? I never get to be surprised myself. I know everything. So one of my greatest joys is to spring the unexpected on my subjects. I get a real charge out of setting it all up, too."

"As you wish, Your Grace," said Martin.

The Great One laughed again. "Oh Martin, cheer up. You play a major role in the next part of this saga, you know"

"Yes, Majesty. I know you always speak the truth," Martin answered.

"My dear Keeper," said the Majesty. "Take heart. I chose you and young Barry to carry this out. Both of you are exactly where you are supposed to be right now."

Martin shook his head. He was beginning to wish he was several galaxies away from this "mission."

ABOUT THE AUTHOR:

Hello, Reader! Thanks for checking out my books. I hope you will enjoy the series. I am C. M. Henderson, Author of <u>THE BLOOD JEWEL</u>, Book I of *The Shomara Diaries*. My goal is to share my love of reading with you. I particularly love writing for kids. For starters, I used to be a kid myself. Okay, so that was back in the Jurassic Age, but hey. I know kids. I was even the oldest in a family of five children. Later, as a teacher, I taught thousands of children from all age groups.

But why middle grade? Well, because they are the "wonder years." I remember them like they were yesterday. It was the time in my life when I fell in love with reading.

Originally from Canada, I spent my first fourteen years in southern Ontario, the daughter of a school principal. My mom was a stay-at-home domestic engineer with a firm hand on the throttle of my little life. (Boy, howdy!)

Both my parents loved to read and they passed on that love to me. One of my favorite memories as a child was when our family would all gather around Dad and he read to us from the Reader's Digest. He could never make it all the way through Laughter Is the Best or Humor in Uniform without having to stop and catch his breath he'd be laughing so hard. And we all held our sides right along with him.

Though our home was a happy one, it was often a rackety, bustling affair. (Remember, *five* kids!) I often yearned for peace and quiet. But there was never any retreat from the noise until one day . . . I read a good book. All of a sudden, everything around me went *silent*. It was the best escape ever! I could get so lost in a novel that my mother said she 'could run a freight train through the middle of the living room, and I wouldn't bat an eye.' She was right.

My appetite for books became insatiable. I raided the library at least once a week devouring the Tarzan series, the Hardy Boys, Cherry Ames, Nancy Drew, and Anne of Green Gables. I could never get enough. By ninth grade, I was reading hefty volumes like Quo Vadis. Through stories, I could run away to far-off cultures and experience life through characters that became as real to me as my own family.

Though my career was in music—I taught both privately and in the public schools—I discovered, quite by accident, that I had a heart for writing. Here is how it happened. I needed a way to spice up some less-than-interesting classical music in my curriculum so I began jotting down little fantasies to read before introducing the listening pieces. The kids loved them—but my strategy backfired. My classes started refusing to hear the music unless Mrs. Henderson first read her story!

In the process of generating these little stories I noticed something: every time I sat down to write, *time disappeared*. I would even forget to eat or sleep. In fact, my new career has taken me back to the same delight of my childhood days when I fell in love with books.

Writing The Shomara Diaries series continues to be a labor of love. But my greatest joy? My greatest joy is watching folks lose themselves in my fantasy world. There's nothing like it.

C. M. Henderson

Made in the USA
San Bernardino, CA
20 September 2014